"Knowledge is power."
—*Francis Bacon*

17-year-old Johanna Charette is the youngest curator ever selected to oversee the Library of Illumination, a centuries old, hard-to-find institution where the books literally come to life. She accepts the job knowing surprises and danger lurk in her future. She also knows, in case of trouble, having an assistant can be invaluable, so she hires 16-year-old Jackson Roth to give her a hand with the day-to-day operation of the library. Jackson gets off to a rocky start, and Johanna worries that he's not going to work out, however, he manages to prove his mettle over the next few months. Besides, he's kind of cute and a lot of fun, and he really has a good heart.

Johanna is levelheaded and mature in her decisions. She keeps the library operating on an even keel. Jackson is quick thinking and intrepid, and he relies on his wits when trouble arises. Unfortunately, his derring-do is also one of the reasons why they sometimes land in awkward situations. And it shouldn't be any surprise when his wanton curiosity sparks a journey to a distant realm where they end up with front row seats to what's destined to become—a war of the worlds.

BOOKS IN THIS SERIES

The Library of Illumination
First book in the series
The Curator

The Library of Illumination:
Book Two
Doubloons

The Library of Illumination:
Book Three
The Orb

The Library of Illumination:
Book Four
Casanova

The Library of Illumination:
Book Five
Portals

Chronicles: The Library of Illumination
Books One through Five

The Library of Illumination:
Book Six
The Overseer (2014)

CHRONICLES: THE LIBRARY OF ILLUMINATION

C. A. PACK

Artiqua Press

http//:www.artiquapress.com

Artiqua Press

Artiqua Press
www.ArtiquaPress.com

This is a work of fiction. The characters, incidents, and dialogue are products of the author's imagination and are not to be construed as real. Any resemblance to actual events or persons, living or dead, is entirely coincidental.

No part of this publication may be reproduced, distributed, or transmitted in any form or by any means, including photocopying, recording, or other electronic, digital or mechanical methods, without the prior written permission of the publisher, except in the case of brief quotations embodied in critical reviews and certain other noncommercial uses permitted by copyright law. For permission requests, write to the publisher, addressed "Attention: Permissions Coordinator," at the address below.

Artiqua Press
Westbury, NY 11590

PUBLISHING HISTORY
ARTIQUA PRESS TRADE PAPERBACK EDITION
MARCH 2014

PORTALS

THE LIBRARY OF ILLUMINATION

ISBN-13: 978-0-9835723-8-1

To all those who loves to hold a book in their hand and immerse themselves in the written word, this book is for you.

LOI

CHAPTER ONE

JACKSON CARRIED AN armful of returned books to a dimly lit alcove in the Library of Illumination's cupola. It was a special area reserved for some of the library's quirkier offerings. The teen enjoyed reading the various titles, but after looking inside *The Pop-Up Book of Phobias*, he refrained from opening any of the others. Unleashing overpowering arachnophobia is not fun.

He hesitated as he shelved *Lamb: The Gospel According to Biff, Christ's Childhood Pal*. When he had some time, he would have to come back and take a closer look at that one. He wasn't sure what a few of the other books were about. *Prodigiorum Ac Ostentorums Chronicon* was Greek to him, and he had never heard of *The Codex Seraphinianus*. There was the *Egyptian Book of the Dead*, but there was no way he would ever open that one. And no library would be complete without *Ripley Scrowle* and *Prophecies* by M. Michel de Nostredame. *I wonder if Johanna has unenchanted versions of these.*

The recess appeared shadowy, which mystified Jackson because there was an octagonal window at the end of the alcove. It should have allowed light to flow into the library, but the aging etched glass looked frosted and did not permit a view of the outside.

Jackson shook his head. *Something's not right here.* After shelving the last book, he ran down the cupola stairs and shouted, "Illumination," as he took off out the front door. He looked up at the area where he thought the alcove should be located, but didn't see a window.

He tried circumnavigating the library, which wasn't an easy thing to do considering it had no side alleys, so he had to go around the entire block. Still, he couldn't find that particular octagonal window.

Johanna stood waiting by the door when he walked back in. "What's wrong?"

"Nothing, really."

"Where did you disappear to? I thought somebody died, the way you ran out of here."

"The thing is," Jackson mused, "there's a little window in the alcove where we keep the wacko books, which should be visible from outside, but there's no corresponding window out there."

"Repeat after me, there is no such thing as a wacko book. And there has to be a window. If there's one in here, you should be able to see it from out there."

He grabbed her arm and dragged her out the door. "Look up. If the cupola stairs are near the center of the building and the weirdo-book alcove is on the left, the window should be right there." He pointed. "But it's not."

"Wait. That doesn't make any sense. I've got to go back inside and get my bearings." Johanna went all the way up to the cupola, and then carefully traced her way back down and out the front entrance. "You're right. There should be a window there. I guess the one in the alcove is a fake."

"Why would anyone put a fake window in a library hundreds of years ago?"

"I don't know. It doesn't make sense."

"So I'm thinking, maybe it hides a safe and there are piles of gold in there."

Johanna covered her face with both her hands for a few seconds. When she finally looked up, she said, "That is so ... you."

"C'mon. Let's go look." Jackson grabbed her hand and dragged her back to the alcove window.

For several minutes, they stood and stared at the octagonal wooden frame filled with radiating triangles of leaded glass. "I never realized you couldn't see outside," she said. "I wonder what would happen if we cleaned it."

"Your wish is my command." Jackson practically flew down the cupola stairs to retrieve some rags and a spray bottle of glass cleaner from the utility room.

He returned before Johanna had a chance to miss him. He doused the fabric with cleanser and started rubbing the window. Grime came off on the rag, but the view remained obscured. "It's not a window, so no matter how much I clean it, we won't be able to see through it. I'm telling you, it's hiding something."

"Forget it. There's no way we're going to open it," Johanna said dismissively. "Besides, it looks like it's painted in place."

Jackson tried prying it with his fingers. "Wait ..."

He bolted down the stairs again, and returned a few minutes later with a box cutter. This time his breathing sounded a little more ragged. The cupola steps spiraled straight to the first floor—five stories below—with no exits along the way. Running up and down the staircase several times took a toll on the teen, but not enough to derail his overall enthusiasm. He used the box cutter to slice through the paint that sealed the window to the wall. Once he had cut through all eight sides, he tried to pry the window open again.

"I don't think it's going to open," Johanna said. "Let's quit before you hurt yourself."

"No. This is my mystery, and I want to solve it." He ran downstairs again, and returned with a crowbar.

"No." Johanna grabbed it away from him. "I can't allow you to destroy library property."

"I'll fix anything I destroy."

"Oh really?"

"Yeah. Ask my mother. I'm the one who fixes everything around the house. If I destroy this, I'll fix it and you can deduct the cost of materials from my salary."

"I don't know ..."

Before she had a chance to think it over, Jackson jammed the edge of the crowbar under the window frame and tried to pry it off.

"They must have screwed this thing in place, because it's not giving way. Nails would have pulled out by now." He inspected the wood, but it had been covered by so many centuries of paint and varnish, he couldn't determine where the screws would be. "I need to give this one more try." He grimaced as he shoved the crowbar against the window frame with all his strength. Little beads of sweat broke out on his brow, and a vein in his forehead became clearly visible. He stopped to rest for a moment.

"This is crazy," Johanna said. "It's not going to open. There is no safe behind it. Why are you wasting your energy?"

"It's my energy to waste. Besides, I think I can do it this time." Jackson took a deep breath before applying force against the crowbar. "Aarrgghh!" He grunted as he worked to remove the window frame. *Crack.* A one-inch chunk of wood broke away and dropped to the floor.

"At this rate, you should be done in less than a week."

"Not funny. The least you could do is help me. If we both pushed against the crowbar, I bet it would work."

Johanna sighed. "Okay. Whenever you're ready."

"On the count of three. One ... two ... three." They pushed as hard as they could, but nothing happened.

"Okay," he said reluctantly. "Forget it. I'm throwing in the towel."

"It's not like opening it is going to provide any illumination for this space."

As soon as Johanna uttered the word *illumination*, the octagonal window flew open, and the great outdoors did *not* appear on the other side.

Johanna and Jackson each held their breath for a few seconds.

"You said, 'illumination.'"

As soon as he repeated the word, the two of them were sucked through the portal to a place that was extremely strange, yet eerily familiar. It had the same proportions as the Library of Illumination, but instead of books, row upon row of crystal obelisks lined the narrow shelves. They walked out of the alcove and found the surrounding area laid out exactly like the cupola in their library.

"Where are we?" Johanna whispered.

"It looks like a mirror image of the library, but it's got all these tall, pointy things where the books should be."

"Let's get out of here."

"Wait. I want to see where we are."

Johanna shook her head. "I don't think that's a good idea."

"Where's your spirit of adventure? Where's your plucky, can-do attitude? Where's your imagination?"

"It's my imagination that's telling me to go back where we belong."

"Okay, see you later." Jackson said it breezily as he walked to the cupola steps. "Look." He pointed to a strange symbol embedded in the stair post. "This must be *their* equivalent of the number one. I'll never understand why this floor is considered the *first* level, while the main floor is called level five. It doesn't make any sense."

Johanna walked closer to look at the symbol. "I read about it in Mal's diary," she explained, as Jackson grabbed her hand and pulled her down the stairs. "The cupola is the highest level, so it's number one. Think of it like winning a prize. If you win first place, that's the highest you can go. It's *first*, not *fifth*. With that in mind, it makes sense that the window level right below it is the second level. Those massive arched windows were designed to flood the library with light, although the light in this library is sort of unearthly."

"Yeah, like they're lighting the place for a horror film."

"The third level," she continued, "is the halo. It's just a single layer of shelves on a narrow balcony that overlook the floors below. The fourth level is known as the residence level."

"That's a no-brainer, considering that's where your apartment is."

"And the main floor is the fifth level."

They had reached the main reading room. The circulation desk was the same familiar shape, but the shelves still held crystal obelisks.

JOHANNA REACHED FOR Jackson's hand and relaxed when his warm fingers curled around her own.

He pulled her toward the curator's staircase. It was right by the residence, and it was the staircase they used most often. There were also stone steps built into the foundation near the front door that linked the main reading room to the residence level, but that staircase was rarely used because the books closest to it were about obscure musical tonalities with archaic chord-scale relationships—not a trendy topic. The more popular books on music could be found closer to the curator's apartment.

Johanna studied the main floor as they walked across it. The reading room looked downright uncomfortable. The furniture, or what she supposed was furniture, included an assortment of oddly shaped surfaces dwarfed by the thousands of obelisks crowding the shelves. She looked up. The windows, opaque with grime, looked like they hadn't been cleaned in a millennium. It looked like their library, and yet it wasn't their library.

"Let's go up to the next floor," Jackson urged.

"I don't think that's such a good idea," she whispered.

"Why? I don't think there's anyone here."

"How can you be so sure?"

"Do you hear anybody?"

"Maybe they're in the antechamber, binding books."

"What books?"

"All right, they're polishing the crystal."

"One more level isn't going to hurt." He tried to pull her up the steps.

"No," Johanna said, wrenching her hand away from his. "That's the residence level, and I have no intention of finding out who lives there."

"I hadn't thought of that. Wouldn't it be cool to see how your other half lives?"

"My other half!"

"Shhh. They'll hear you," he whispered.

"Exactly." She turned to go back.

"I'm going without you." He quickly climbed to the next level.

Johanna couldn't help herself. Instead of returning to the cupola, she walked into the middle of the reading room, where she could keep an eye on him. The balconies on the residence level were fairly visible, and Johanna followed Jackson's progress until he stopped just outside the curator's apartment. She waved to get his attention, but either he didn't see her or he ignored her. *Why does he have to be so difficult? He's playing with fire.*

JACKSON BEGAN TO notice subtle differences in the obelisks, not just in their height and width but on their surfaces as well. At first he thought they were dusty, but on closer examination he saw that they had subtle etchings on them, like a design, or another language, or code. He looked down at Johanna and waved at her to come up.

She adamantly shook her head from side to side.

She's so stubborn. He felt sure they had discovered something monumental about this library, but he didn't know what it was. He wanted to discuss it with her, but knew if he walked back down the stairs, she would interpret that as a signal they could leave and would head back up to the cupola. *There has to be a way I can get her up here.*

JOHANNA'S IMPATIENCE GREW. *Why tempt fate? Why can't he wait until I ask Mal about this?* She needed to know what to expect. She motioned for Jackson to return. He held up one finger, as if to say, *wait a minute.* She didn't want to waste another moment. *I should just leave, and if he wants to follow, fine.* She raised her arm to wave goodbye, but could not stop herself from shouting "No" when Jackson reached for the crystal lever that opened the bookcase-door to the residence. He looked down at her and waved.

She watched in horror as a dark tentacle shot out of the residence, wrapped itself around Jackson's neck, and dragged him inside. Her heart nearly stopped. Jackson had been caught trespassing, but by what? And who knew what kind of trouble he had gotten himself into? Her fear was for him rather than herself. She practically flew up the stairs to the residence. When she got there, the shelf that disguised the entrance had swung back into position and the crystal lever was gone. She began hammering on the wall behind the obelisks, hoping for Jackson's sake that there would be strength in numbers—hopefully, two against one. After not receiving any response to her pounding, she decided the best way to get attention would be to make some *real* noise. She picked up the closest obelisk and hurled it across the aisle, sending it crashing into a shelf crammed with more of the literary crystals.

Instantly, the balcony filled with swirling fog. An odd being that looked like he had been formed out of molten gold rose from the depths of the mist. A blue diamond band surrounded the entity's head, and lightning bolts shot out of it at varying intervals. It began communicating in a language Johanna could not understand. Even the translation app on the iPad would not have been able to help her. The words sounded more like grunts—"iks" and "ogs," "nnhs" and "utzs."

She shrank back against the shelf that had held the obelisk. She suddenly realized she couldn't calmly close a book and make the apparition go away. There was no book to close, and the obelisk that she had sent sailing through a sea of air had broken into tiny pieces. She thought about how she would feel if someone had trashed one of her precious books. Her shoulders sagged. She had done something childish, something to gain attention, although not the kind of attention she wanted. In the process she had destroyed something precious, if not to her, to someone else. Not to mention she could be electrocuted at any moment.

Before she could give it any more thought, something wrapped around her neck and dragged her into the residence. The sudden loss of oxygen coupled with surprise caused Johanna to black out. When she came to, she saw Jackson standing in the middle of the room.

"I knew you'd come," he said.

She struggled to her feet, choking on the oily mist that enveloped her. She looked around, but couldn't see much in the hazy darkness. "Where's ..."

"He went out after dragging you in."

"Come on, then, let's get out of here."

"I'd love to, but I can't move."

"What do you mean, you can't move?" She took a step toward him, afraid that she, too, might be unable to move, but if that were true, she would have never been able to get up off the floor. She reached for his hand. *Zap.* She felt electrified, in a bad way.

"Force field ..." they said in unison.

"I have to get you out of here." She thought of how they had handled the force field surrounding the blue orb. "Illumination."

"Uurrgg." Jackson gurgled and squirmed. He suddenly looked like he would choke to death.

"Delumination," she cried out.

He loudly gasped, taking in great gulps of air.

"Can you move?"

"No."

"I was hoping 'delumination' would work."

His body relaxed. He took another deep breath, then a step. "The second one worked, which is good, because for a moment I thought you might kill me."

"I guess it's like the little window. You have to say it twice for it to work. Anyway, we need to get out of here. But I did something stupid. I broke one of their obelisks ... on purpose, and it released an odd being with lightning coming out of its ... head. Since the obelisk is broken, I don't know what they're going to do to contain it. Whoever captured you may still be out there."

"Unless it took the obelisk to the antechamber to glue it back together," Jackson speculated.

"There must be something it can do to repair it. Anyway, just be prepared for anything when I open the door."

"Frit."

"Excuse me?"

"Just a family saying. My brother, Chris, once said 'friggan shit' in front of my mother, and she had a conniption. So he got into the habit of condensing it into 'frit', and now we all say it, even my mother and my little sister."

"That's nice. Can we get back to the problem at hand?" She had no idea what kind of beings they were dealing with. "Do you think they're human?"

"My mother and my sister?"

"Don't joke. I'm talking about whatever captured you."

"I don't think so. I didn't get a chance to pay much attention to what captured me, but I can tell you, it had an iron grip."

"Just be prepared to run. But—and this is a big 'but'—if we can't outrun it, we shouldn't go back the way we came, because we don't want it following us back into *our library*."

"How are we supposed to stop it from doing that?"

"I don't know."

"I wonder if there are any more windows to nowhere, in any of the other alcoves."

"What good would that do us? We might just end up in a library that's scarier than this one."

"Yeah, but there's usually no one up in the cupola. We could just hide out until we think it's safe."

"Unless whatever is chasing us follows us there." She sighed. "Let's just make a run for it and try to get back home. Ready?"

They each took a deep breath. Jackson nodded to Johanna, and she hit the lever that opened the door to the residence. No one was there. They tiptoed down to the main level and across the floor, and then broke into a run—straight up the stairs to the cupola. They didn't slow down to see if anything was behind them. They couldn't afford to waste precious time.

"Illumination," Johanna cried as they ran into

the alcove. They hit the wall hard but remained in the same unfamiliar library. She could hear someone, or something, stomping up the cupola stairs.

"What are we going to do now?" Jackson asked.

Johanna thought about him being trapped behind the force field in the residence, and how she had said the wrong thing at first. "Delumination."

Nothing happened.

"Why did you say, 'Delumination'?" As soon as Jackson repeated her command, they felt themselves swoosh away to another place.

"Oh my God," Jackson exclaimed.

"What?" she cried, looking around in a panic.

"It's the *Pop-Up Book of Phobias.*" He smiled at her, and in a singsong voice said, "Honey, we're ho-ome."

"Maybe not," Johanna whispered.

"What do you mean?"

She looked down.

Jackson immediately knew what she meant. The floors were as transparent as glass.

—LOI—

LOI

CHAPTER TWO

"Do you see anyone?" Johanna whispered.

"No, but even if I did, how often does anybody look up at the cupola?"

A chime went off, followed by the whirring sound of the front wall sliding open four stories below. Johanna and Jackson stooped down to peer through the transparent floor. They saw a large man covered with curly, red hair stomp into the library. He wore a caftan of rich, blue silk emblazoned with a bright gold design. "FURST," he screamed.

He walked over to the circulation desk and relentlessly rang a bell until a small man, also covered with curly, red hair, came running from a back room. He, too, wore a caftan, but it only reached as far as his knobby knees and appeared to be made of plain sackcloth.

"At your service, I am." The smaller man pulled the bell out of the larger one's hand and placed it out of reach, behind the desk.

"The book ordered, I want."

"Here, it is not."

"On Tuesday, you promised."

"Here, it is not," the little man said a tiny bit louder.

"It, where is?"

"Of our region, outside."

"Beyond us, it is?"

"By force, taken."

"Get it back, you will?"

"An army, I would need."

"Stop, this must."

"An army, I would need," the little man said a tiny bit louder.

"To the council, I will speak."

"With my regard, go forth."

"Furst," the larger man said, nodding his head.

"Dungen," the smaller man replied, nodding to the big man's back as he exited the library. When the wall slid back into place, the little man retreated.

Johanna and Jackson watched as he walked back in the direction of the antechamber.

"How odd," Johanna whispered.

"Did you understand any of that?"

"No. And I don't want to. I want to get back home."

"How are we going to do that?"

She gave it some thought. "I think we ran up the wrong alcove and through a different window."

"I'd be more than happy to look in the other alcoves to see if there are more windows. Too bad the walls aren't made out of glass."

"Don't do anything foolish," she warned.

"I won't." On impulse, he kissed the tip of her

nose and then winked as he slipped away.

The cupola formed a triquetra, three intersecting ellipses intertwined with a circle. The winding aisles snaked like a puzzle, and the points of the ellipses formed the alcoves. Johanna saw Jackson only for a second, as he crossed the far side of the cupola. She sighed with relief when he finally returned to where she waited. "So?"

"There's an identical hazy window at the end of each alcove."

"You're kidding ..."

"Not only that. There are similar windows in some of the hallways. That opens up a lot of possibilities, and we can only guess at picking the right one."

"From what you could see, did it look like we're in the wrong alcove?"

He shook his head. "As far as I can tell, this is the alcove we started out from."

"Great." The word belied her feeling of frustration.

"Look, when we ran in what we thought was the right direction, we ended up here, not back at home. So I'm thinking, even if we go through this same window, we shouldn't end up back in scary town."

"I think I'd rather take my chances talking to the little red-haired man. Maybe he knows something about these windows."

"And if he starts chasing us?"

"We run."

"Okay, let's go."

"Quietly."

Jackson nodded.

They crept down the stairs, and Johanna pulled Jackson toward the circulation desk. "Let's ring, so it doesn't look like we're invading his space."

"Where's the bell?"

She made a face. "I'm pretty sure he put it on a shelf." She walked around the circulation desk and slipped inside the gate leading behind the counter. She saw the bell and grabbed it, but didn't get a chance to ring it.

"Behind my circulation desk, what business have you?" The curator practically roared at her, not at all like the meek little man who had just cowered before his much-larger kinsman.

Johanna placed the bell on the counter. "I'm Johanna Charette, curator of the Library of Illumination ... uh ... another Library of Illumination. We came in through a window in one of the alcoves, and we're wondering if some sort of map exists that can help us get back to our own library."

The man just stared at her.

She gave it another try. "We're not supposed to be here. Can you help us?"

"Operating, the portals are." He said it barely above a whisper, with a look of dread upon his face.

"We mean you no harm," Johanna continued. "We just want to go home."

"Use the portals, why did you?"

"Know what they are, we did not," Jackson broke in.

Johanna poked him. "Why are you talking like that?"

"Because that's how he speaks. It's almost like Yoda from *Star Wars*."

"Want to go, where do you?" the man asked.

"Where are we now?"

"The Realm of Dramatica, this Library of Illumination is in."

That piqued Jackson's interest. "You're a realm? That's so cool!"

"A realm, you must be from," the curator said decisively.

Jackson looked at Johanna. "What realm are we from?"

"I have no idea."

"Of your library, what are the properties?"

"Do you mean the different levels of the books? Mostly twos and threes, although we recently had a four, and Casanova caused all kinds of havoc."

"Come alive, do your books?"

"Yes."

"Here, wait."

He disappeared into the antechamber, and returned a moment later with a large, tattered book, which had a heavy, metal padlock. He held the palm of his right hand about an inch above the lock, and it popped open.

Furst slowly turned the pages. Jackson leaned over to see what he was reading, but could not see any words. He whispered in Johanna's ear, "The pages are blank."

She smiled. "That's because you're not the curator."

"Right."

"Found it, I have," Furst said, with a satisfied smile. "Of the Eleventh Realm, Johanna Charette, you are. Fantasia, it is called."

"Really?"

"Fantasia? Fantastic. At least, I think it's fantastic that you found us," Jackson said. "The Eleventh Realm, huh?"

"And you said we are now in ...?" Johanna asked.

"In the Sixth Realm, Dramatica is."

"Wow," Jackson said. "We traveled five realms."

Johanna shook her head. "Like that means

anything to you."

"Well, at least this isn't like the scary library with the guy with the tentacles."

Furst paled. "Another library, you have been to?"

"Yeah. A scary place with obelisks instead of books, that's run by someone or something with tentacles."

Furst consulted the gold book.

Johanna watched his hand start to tremble. He looked at her with horror in his eyes. "Terroria, that is, the Twelfth Realm. Talk to the Library Council, I must. The Two Millennia War, Terroria started."

"Why did they start a war?" Johanna inquired.

"To take over all the libraries, they wanted. Very serious, this is."

"Can you tell us how to get back to our own library?" Jackson asked.

"Go, you cannot. Talk to the Library Council, you must."

JACKSON GNAWED ON his thumbnail. He leaned close to Johanna. "How long do you think they're going to keep us?"

"You actually look worried."

"It's just that I promised Logan I'd be there tomorrow for our community-service project. He's depending on me."

"You didn't tell me you're working on a project."

"Yeah, we have to do it to graduate. Logan and I got some of the local home-improvement stores to donate materials, and we're going to fix up the outside of Old Lady Caruthers's place, which is falling apart."

"It sounded wonderful until you ruined it all by calling her 'Old Lady' Caruthers."

"Point taken. Anyway, like I told you before, I'm handy around the house. So we're going to paint the exterior and replace the shutters, and Cassie's father is a contractor, so he volunteered to help us rebuild the porch. Chris is getting a few of his friends to chop up the broken front walkway, and Cassie's dad is going to show us how to pour concrete. Plus, Cassie and Brittany got the Mothers' Club to donate flowers and stuff that they're going to plant in front of the new porch and along the sidewalk. It's a lot of work, but we're hoping to finish it all in one day. I've got to be there. We made a commitment."

Johanna was impressed by the scope of work Jackson and Logan had taken on. Plus they managed to get promises and donations from others, to make the revitalization project a success. "You should shoot video of it and put it to music, so you can upload it to the Internet."

"I won't be able to shoot anything, because I'll be too busy working. But *you* can volunteer to shoot it." He put his arm around her. "It'll be fun."

"First, we have to get out of here," she said pragmatically.

"The next time I come up with a bright idea, like opening a library window, you have my permission to fire me."

"Thanks. I'll remember that."

It did not take long for the Dramatican Library Council to convene. Their library had a giant bell in an open tower over the entryway, and the peals immediately drew council members from all over the city. They dropped whatever they were doing to respond to the perceived emergency.

"For five hundred years, the bell has not rung,"

Furst told them. "Great danger, we are in."

The council members stared at Johanna and Jackson as they gathered around a table in Dramatica's version of the executive boardroom. The stone walls and leaded glass windows reminded Johanna of her own library; however, this one had a glass ceiling and a glass table.

Jackson knocked twice on the tabletop. "I like this. It's really cool."

Furst leaned over and whispered, "Secret deals made under the table, it is to prevent."

"Ahhh," Jackson answered.

"Explain," one of the council members demanded.

"Speak, you must," Furst told Johanna.

She stood up and looked at the assembly of people before her. They were all covered with curly red hair and wore caftans of varying degrees of richness. "I'm Johanna Charette, curator of the Library of Illumination on Fantasia." She looked at Furst for reassurance, and he nodded at her. "We found a small window that could not be seen from the outside of our library, and we tried to open it to see what was behind it. When we managed to do that, we were transported to another library, much like our own, except instead of books we found obelisks." This statement incited an increase in murmurings among the Library Council members. "When Jackson"—she pointed to her assistant—"went to find out where we were, someone or something with tentacles imprisoned him and placed him behind a force field." The sound level increased even more. "I saw him get pulled into the residence, but by the time I got there, I couldn't get inside. No one would come to the door, so to get their attention—and this pains me deeply to say—I threw one of their obelisks, breaking it." The murmuring grew quite loud.

"Here now, you are. Get away, how did you?"

She took a deep breath. "I was pulled into the residence after I broke the obelisk, but whatever dragged me inside must have rushed to inspect the damage, without bothering to secure me behind a force field. Jackson was immobilized, but because of something that happened recently in our own library, I managed to say the right thing to get the force field to release him.

"We left the residence and ran up to the cupola, where the window is located. We went back through it, but instead of returning to our own library, we ended up here."

"Through the window, did anyone see you leave?"

"We heard someone coming up the steps, but I don't know if he, or she, or it, saw us disappear through the window."

Torran, the largest of the Library Council members, stood. Gold embroidery covered every inch of his caftan, and jewels encrusted the neckline and edges. He had a deep, resonant voice. "The portals, you have breached."

"So they're like the portals from *Stargate*?" Jackson asked.

"A system of portals that connect all the libraries, it is said there exists. But hidden by the College of Overseers many years ago they were, when the Two Millennia War Terroria started. Seek to take over all the libraries, they did."

"Can you tell us how to get back to our own library?" Johanna asked.

"Breach the portals, we cannot. Know their true directions, we do not. Summon the College of Overseers, we must. Now."

"How do you do that?" Jackson asked.

"The Curator Key, Furst must engage."

Furst turned his head upward and looked through the glass ceiling to the very top of the cupola.

"Easy, it will not be," he mumbled.

"Do it, you must," Torran demanded.

Furst left the room, and the other council members trailed behind him. They talked among themselves as they waited, while the curator descended to a sub-level.

"What's this Curator Key they're talking about?" Jackson asked Johanna.

"I don't know. I could probably ask Mal's diary, but I don't have it with me. I didn't realize we were going on an excursion or precipitating a war."

"Sorry."

They heard scraping and turned to see Furst dragging a large ladder behind him. "Here, let me help you with that," Jackson said, picking up the back of the ladder. "Where are you taking it?"

Furst pointed straight up.

Jackson grimaced. He ended up on the lower end of the ladder as they lugged it up the cupola stairs, toward the highest point in the building.

"Place it across the railings, we must," Furst said, pointing to where he wanted Jackson to carry his end of the ladder. They extended it as far as it would go and laid it horizontally across the rails.

"Now what?"

"A rope, I must get." Furst disappeared down the stairs, pushing through the stream of council members who climbed up to watch. He returned several minutes later with a coil of rope. He tied one end into a lasso and the other around his waist. Then he climbed on top of the ladder.

"Whoa, whoa, whoa, what are you doing?" Jackson called out, grabbing the end of the ladder.

"Reach the hook with the rope, I must."

Furst started to crawl across the makeshift wooden bridge that now spanned the open space in the middle of the cupola. He moved very slowly. Jackson couldn't tell if Furst wobbled because of nerves, or because the ladder wasn't strong enough to hold his weight. None of Furst's countrymen moved to help him accomplish his task.

"Johanna," Jackson called out. "Can you grab the other end of the ladder and hold it still?"

"Will do," she responded, grabbing the opposite side.

The two teens watched as Furst shakily stood up in the middle of the ladder. He took the section of rope that he had tied into a lasso and threw it toward the uppermost part of the ceiling. It missed whatever target the curator had hoped it would catch on to, and fell downward, pulling Furst off balance. Everyone gasped as the curator fell. Furst managed to grab on to the edge of the ladder and dangled several stories above the library's main reading room.

—LOI—

LOI

CHAPTER THREE

THE LIBRARY COUNCIL members discussed Furst's dilemma in detail, but not one of them moved to help him.

Jackson climbed onto the edge of the ladder.

"What are you doing?" Johanna screamed.

"Someone's got to save him," he told her. "Hey, I'd appreciate a little help here," he yelled at the council members at large.

One of them, a man in a brown silk caftan without much ornamentation, grabbed hold of Jackson's end of the ladder. The teen crawled out to where Furst clung, all the while praying that the ladder was strong enough to support them both. He straddled the ladder when he reached the curator and locked his ankles together. Grabbing Furst by his arms, Jackson pulled him up high enough so the Dramatican could get a better grip.

Jackson contemplated his next move. Normally,

he would reach over and grab Furst's waistband to haul him up, but the man wore a caftan. Instead, the teen grabbed the rope Furst had attached to his waist. It had been tied with a slipknot, and Jackson could only reach the part that pulled it loose. As a last resort, the young man grabbed a handful of fabric from Furst's caftan and hauled him up, hoping the man wore underwear, or else Johanna would get an eyeful.

Furst managed to scramble back on the ladder to the cheers of the council members. As he sat catching his breath, he trembled as sweat oozed from every pore.

"What, exactly, are you trying to do?" Jackson asked.

Furst looked up and pointed. "A hook up at the top, there is. Try to lasso it to pull myself up, I did."

"Okay, first things first. Untie that rope from your waist and tie it to the ladder instead." Jackson took the lasso end in his hand. Taking a deep breath, he narrowed his eyes in concentration, and tossed it. Everyone released a collective sigh when the rope missed its mark. Jackson retrieved the line, which now dangled from the ladder, grabbed the lasso again, and thought about how Johanna never missed the trash bin when she free-tossed a wadded-up piece of paper across the length of the circulation desk. *I can do this,* he thought. He stared at the hook. He envisioned the lasso snagging it. He thought about how contacting the College of Overseers could pave the way for them to get back home. He raised his elbow so the noose hung open from his wrist and, without taking his eye off the hook, flung the rope upward. He watched as it climbed, willing it to snag the hook.

"That's what I'm talking about," he screamed, when the rope caught hold.

Enthusiastic shouts and whistles erupted from

the group.

Jackson looked at Furst, who had broken into a wide smile. "What do I need to do when I get up there?"

Furst's face fell. "You cannot. The curator, I am. Contact the college, only the curator can."

"Are you going to be okay doing this?"

"Know, I do not."

"Have you ever climbed a rope before?"

"No."

"We should have knotted the rope before we tossed it," he said, thinking out loud. He looked at Furst, who still looked scared. "Wait here."

Jackson untied the rope from the ladder and climbed to the top of it. He took a moment to study the Curator's Key. It wasn't a key at all, but an intricate dialing mechanism. The odd configuration of brass gears and ivory numbered buttons reminded him of Jules Verne's *Time Machine. I wonder if we have one of these.* Jackson shifted his gaze to the hook. It had been solidly integrated in the framework of the cupola. From up close, it was fairly large. He slowly slid back down to the ladder. "Do you have another rope?"

Furst nodded.

"Do you want to get it?"

Furst turned and tentatively stared at the end of the ladder.

"Better yet," Jackson continued, "tell me where it is, and I'll go and get it, that way you can save your energy for climbing it."

"Sub-level six, it is in. Next to the cellar stairs, it is."

"I'll be right back."

Jackson crawled to the edge of the ladder and jumped down onto the floor of the cupola. He didn't waste any time answering questions. He just ignored them all and ran down the stairs. The buzz level increased, as council members stared at Furst and called out their questions to him.

"Another rope, we need," he answered, not exactly knowing why they needed it.

Jackson returned a couple of minutes later, with the second coil of rope hanging from his shoulder. He crawled back on the ladder and formed a noose on one end and proceeded to tie knots at one-foot intervals. Then he scrambled up the rope that he'd already attached to the ceiling and secured the knotted line to the same hook.

He returned to Furst. "Those knots will keep you from sliding back down as you climb up. Just grab the rope above the knot, pull up your knees, and then wrap the loose end of the rope around one foot and use your other foot to hold it in place. Every time you straighten your legs, you'll be able to reach higher, and you just need to keep doing that until you reach the top."

Furst nodded. He grabbed the rope and used it to pull himself up to a standing position. He reached as high as he could and pulled up his knees as Jackson had advised, but had difficulty wrapping the rope around his foot and using the other foot to hold it in place. After three tries, he returned to a sitting position on the ladder. "Do it, I cannot. Doomed, we are."

Jackson gave it some thought. "You can do it," he said, with a smile. "Try it again."

Furst slowly stood up and grabbed the rope. Jackson stood up as well. When Furst pulled his feet up, Jackson looped the rope around one foot and pushed Furst's other foot into place. "Straighten your legs and move your hands higher," Jackson told him. Furst did, and Jackson climbed the second rope to help the man wrap his foot again. Together, the two men climbed the pair of ropes—student and teacher—until they reached the top.

"Okay, do your thing," Jackson said.

"Afraid to let go, I am," Furst replied, his voice filled with panic.

"You won't fall. I'll hold you in place. Are your feet tight against the rope?"

"Yes."

"Okay." Jackson pulled himself up and wrapped his legs around Furst's waist, holding him in place. "Do what you gotta do."

Furst tentatively let go with one hand and manipulated the dial. Jackson watched as the gears slowly turned, screeching with years of non-use.

"Descend, we must," Furst said nervously.

"Just loosen your grip a little at a time and slide."

Jackson released Furst and slid down the rope. The Dramatican curator slowly made his way down to the ladder, at the bottom of which Jackson waited to guide him in. Above them, the gears continued to turn as the opening in the cupola slowly grew larger. They headed in opposite directions, and when they each reached firm ground, Furst motioned Jackson to help him remove the ladder from the railing and place it out of the way. Then they stood and watched with the others as the cupola yawned wider.

METAL ON METAL clanged thunderously as the gears in Dramatica's cupola locked into place. The crowd gasped when a magnificent white light shot upward from the center medallion embedded in the library floor, straight through the opening in the roof. After a minute, the light stopped as suddenly as it had appeared.

"Now what?" Jackson asked.

"Look," Johanna said, pointing toward the various alcoves. A dozen men—nearly identical in appearance—emerged from the twelve portals. Each, one had a long, white beard and even longer, white hair that touched the floor. They all wore purple robes and matching miter hats.

"A plethora of popes," Jackson whispered.

Johanna jammed her elbow in his side. "Stop," she said under her breath.

Torran addressed the overseers. "Torran, I am, Dean of the Library Council."

🎵 *Who is the curator?* the twelve overseers asked in unison.

Furst pushed forward through the throng of men.

"Furst, I am. Curator." He bowed deeply.

🎵 *There is another.*

Furst looked for Johanna in the crowd and signaled for her to join him.

She walked over to where he stood and addressed the twelve men. "I am Johanna Charette, curator of a library in a different realm."

Ω *Realm Eleven.* She heard the words, as did everyone else, but did not know who spoke them.

She breached the portals on Realm Twelve. We must extract Nero 51."

The light shot up through the portal, and two of the overseers disappeared. When the light suddenly turned off, they retuned, flanking the curator known as Nero 51.

The Dramaticans gasped. Nero 51 had the body of a man, but his feet were larger and flatter—like swollen platypus feet—and he had multiple tentacles for arms that could stretch out to untold lengths. His wide head dipped in the middle, rising on either side over large black eyes that commanded more than half his face. He had a flat nose and a very small mouth.

He made a series of unintelligible sounds. One of the overseers waved his hand, and Nero 51's words instantly became understandable. "Terroria has been invaded," he declared, "and our property maliciously destroyed."

The overseers addressed Johanna. 𝔖 *Why did you breach the portal and destroy library property?*

"We did not know about the portals or how they work. When we were unexpectedly transported to another world, my assistant Jackson wanted to explore it. But he was taken and locked in a force field."

"TAKEN? I did no such thing. I found him trying to break into my residence."

"I wasn't really trying to break into the residence," Jackson volunteered. "I only wanted to get Johanna's attention."

𝔖 *You are Jackson?* the overseers asked in unison.

"Yes."

They all nodded.

"Who is Jackson?" Nero 51 demanded. "A curator?"

𝔖 *A curator-in-training.*

"A curator-in-training who has broken the laws of the Library of Illumination, just like his master." Nero 51 glared at Johanna. "I demand justice, with a trial on Terroria before a jury of Terrorians."

𝔖 *Library law is regulated only by a jury populated by overseers. There will be no jury of Terrorians. But we will acquiesce to your request to have the trial on your home world. It is decided.*

Johanna felt a moment of nausea and realized she had unexpectedly been whisked through the portal to another library. She recognized the structure of the executive boardroom, and knew she was on Terroria when she saw the oily mist swirling in the air. It resembled the atmosphere inside the residence in which she found Jackson. Even here, shelves filled with obelisks of all shapes and sizes lined the walls. She looked around the room to see who had accompanied them to witness the proceedings. The twelve overseers were there, as well as Jackson, Furst, and Nero 51, but she was the only other person in the room. The Dramatican Library Council had been left behind.

𝄞 *Johanna Charette, state you story from the beginning, before breaching the portals.*

Once again, she could not tell where the voice originated. She looked at Jackson, startled to see that he, Furst, and Nero 51 were suspended in what appeared to be tubes of glass.

𝄞 *Do not be alarmed,"* the voice said. *"It is to prevent interruption, or the accidental disclosure of sensitive information not meant for the many.*

Johanna recounted how Jackson had discovered a window in the cupola that would not open and how he was sure there must be something like a safe hidden behind it. She explained how she had been skeptical but allowed him to try to remove the window after he promised to fix anything he broke. She explained how saying the word *Illumination* caused the window to fly open, and how Jackson repeating it had resulted in their transport to Terroria. She stated she was "scared" and her primary goal was to return home, but Jackson had a curious mind and a zest for exploring new places. She recounted everything that happened—from breaking the obelisk to escaping the residence—and finished by telling the overseers how surprised she and Jackson were to find themselves on Dramatica, when all they wanted to do was return home.

She revealed how Furst had explained that there were a dozen realms, plus the home world, Lumina, and that she came from Fantasia, Realm Eleven, which she hadn't known.

An overseer nodded, and Johanna found herself inside a glass tube. She watched as Jackson answered the overseers' questions, but could not hear what was said.

Jackson had a similar version of what had happened, except he gave more detail about being captured by Nero 51.

"It felt like a steel cable had wrapped around my arms, and when I saw all the tentacles he had, I was surprised he didn't wrap them around my legs as well, because I kicked as hard as I could, trying to get away. But then he reached for this huge weapon that looked like a rocket launcher, threw me against the wall, and fired it at me. I found myself locked behind a force field and couldn't move. He started clicking and whirring at me, but I couldn't tell what he was saying. I just knew he meant business, considering the number of weapons he had stacked up across the room. If that guy's going to war, I don't want to be the enemy."

Jackson found himself back inside the glass tube and watched as Nero 51 approached the overseers.

"THIS IS AN outrage," the Terrorian said in a low-pitched, threatening tone. "Those two *curators*," he sneered, "invaded my library and wreaked havoc. It is against library law. I demand that they be executed for breaking the peace of a million millennia."

Furst was the last person to be interrogated. He spoke about how he had first found Johanna behind the circulation desk holding the bell, and how she said she was back there because the bell was not on the desk. He stated that she spoke the truth, because he had hidden the bell after Dungen gave him a headache by ringing it nonstop.

He was mystified that Johanna did not know anything about the various realms, but said, other than that, she seemed very knowledgeable about the layout of the library and its inner workings.

He talked about his decision to ask the Library Council for permission to contact the Board of Overseers, and that once the decision was made, how Jackson helped him climb to the dial at the top of the portal. He also detailed how the teen had saved his life when he lost his balance and nearly fell to his death.

Like the others, Furst was returned to a soundproof holding tube after his testimony.

After much deliberation, the College of Overseers agreed their decision would depend on the testimony of Johanna's mentor, whom they instantly summoned to corroborate the information they had been given. Mal was escorted to Terroria through one of the portals.

§ *Malcolm Trees?*

"Yes."

§ *It is said your charge had no knowledge of the confluence of realms. Did you not teach her?*

"I did not. I thought her too young to fully comprehend the importance of the information when she first became curator of the library. She is, by far, the youngest person ever to assume that role, although it must be noted, she has admirably mastered the proficiencies necessary to run such a, shall we say, *dynamic* institution. I had arranged for the provenance of the library system to be apportioned to her within the text of my eternal diary, which I know she refers to frequently. I had scheduled it to start in her twenty-first year. She is not even nineteen years old, and I did not want her youth to influence the possibility that she might overlook the importance of our history."

§ *This would bear out the testimony of Furst, who claims she entered Dramatica without knowledge of the realms or her place within them.*

"I am sorry to admit that I have been remiss."

§ *The boy, Jackson, is a curator-in-training?*

"Yes. Johanna hired him to help out at the library. After I witnessed his devotion to her and to the library, I—quite unknown to them—took the necessary steps to have the young man designated a curator-in-training. Like Johanna, his background makes him highly suitable for the position. Together, I believe they will grow into all that the job demands."

§ *You see them as equals, then?*

"Not exactly. The girl is intelligent and pragmatic, with excellent business sense and a love of literature. She is a natural-born leader of the levelheaded variety. Jackson, on the other hand, takes risks Johanna would never take. While this may seem foolhardy at times, his bravery, geniality, and ability to take charge of difficult situations and foresee their outcomes complement her leadership by making Johanna push her boundaries past what is comfortable. I believe they can accomplish great things together. In light of the rumored build-up of arms and unrest in some of the realms, I see them as the light of the future."

§ You have ascertained, then, the increasing possibility of conflict within the realms?

"Yes. It is said the Terrorians are bartering ancient obelisks for weapons."

§ It would be detected.

"Not if the obelisks were replaced by counterfeits."

There was a moment of silence. *§ That is all.*

Mal was escorted back to his point of origin.

—LOI—

LOI

CHAPTER FOUR

❖Recount the charges *against Johanna Charette.*

ᴪ *Charge: Portal Breach.*

❖*Acquitted: She had no knowledge of their existence.*

⬥ *Duly noted.*

ᴪ *Charge: Destruction of LOI Property.*

❖*Guilty: Johanna admitted to destroying property.*

⬥ *Duly noted.*

❖*Recount the charges against Jackson Roth.*

ᴪ *Charge: Portal Breach.*

❖*Acquitted: He had no knowledge of their existence.*

⬥ *Duly noted.*

ᴪ *Charge: Trespass.*

❖*Acquitted: As a LOI curator-in-training, it is impossible to trespass on any LOI property.*

⬥ *Duly noted.*

Ψ *Charge: Illegal Entry of a Residence.*

❖ *Acquitted: The boy was pulled inside and detained by the resident.*

♠ *Duly noted.*

✠ *Johanna must be punished for the destruction of property.*

★ *Extenuating circumstances existed. Nero 51 ignored her communication, thus inviting the use of unorthodox methods to get his attention.*

◍ *She broke the obelisk to save the boy, not knowing what fate awaited him, due to her ignorance of the realms.*

❖ *She must pay for her transgression. She is from Fantasia, based on Earth. It is decreed she work the equivalent of three Earth days on Terroria to repay the loss.*

Σ *Nero 51 will condemn the judgment as too light.*

❖ *Nero 51 is not an overseer.*

π *Johanna Charette will not like the judgment.*

❖ *Johanna Charette must pay for willful destruction of library property. And we need her to serve time on Terroria.*

❊ *Your decision, perhaps, is based on the boy's testimony about weapons, as well as other rumors that have come to light ...*

§ *Ahhh ... the counterfeits.*

❖ *You are correct.*

≈ *And the electromagnetic waves?*

❖ *We continue to monitor them.*

◍ *And the boy, Jackson?*

❖ *He must remain on Earth to curate the Fantasian library.*

Ω *Shall we seal the portals?*

❖ *No. Johanna Charette must be able to return to*

her realm.

■ *What if Nero 51 uses them to wage war?*

❖*That is to be expected, and countered.*

The tubes vanished, and the four curators stood before the College of Overseers.

❖*All charges have been acquitted, save one.*

Nero 51 took a threatening step forward. "How could all charges have been acquitted? I demand retribution."

❖*All charges, save one.*

"And what charge is that?" The Terrorian sneered.

❖*Johanna Charette, you have been found guilty of the willful destruction of LOI property. You are sentenced to work in the service of the library on Terroria for three Earth days.*

"No!" Nero 51 roared. "I do not want her on my world. She is a spy and must be executed!"

❖*Nero 51, Johanna Charette has been sentenced to a period of service on your world. As a ward of Terroria for that given period of time, you must guarantee her safety, or lose all rights as curator of your realm.*

Nero 51 huffed and puffed like he was about to explode.

"If she's going there, I'm going with her," Jackson interjected. "It's my fault she broke the obelisk."

❖*No. Jackson Roth, you have been acquitted of all charges. In the absence of Johanna Charette, you must assume the duties as curator of the Library of Illumination in the realm of Fantasia.*

"You can't let her go to Terroria alone."

❖*It is the finding of the College of Overseers and cannot be overturned. Johanna Charette, you have an equal amount of time to prepare for your sentence: three*

Earth days. We will send an escort to accompany you to Terroria when the moment has arrived.

The College of Overseers stood in unison.

§ *Johanna Charette, Jackson Roth, Furst, accompany us. We will return you to your home worlds before we seal the portals,* the overseers said in unison.

"This is an outrage!" Nero 51 screamed at their retreating number. "I will not stand for it!"

JOHANNA AND JACKSON found themselves back in the alcove of oddities. "Do you think we're really home?" Jackson asked.

Johanna stooped and retrieved a chunk of their wood window frame from the floor. "Yes."

"You can't go to Terroria alone."

"I have to. You heard what the College of Overseers said."

"That Nero guy has it in for you. He wants to execute you."

"He can't without losing his curatorship, and I have the feeling that it's something he doesn't want to lose. So I'll be fine. I'll polish a few obelisks. I'll wash a few windows. Whatever."

"Who's that guy they brought in at the end?"

"Mal."

"That's Mal? Really? He looked so different."

"That's because you met him when he was only one hundred forty years old."

Jackson took a moment to think about what she had just said. "Why do you think they called him there?"

"I don't know, but I have every intention of asking him ... or at least his diary."

"Are you going to do that now?"

"Right now, all I want is a slice of pizza."

"Since I got you into this, I'll treat."

She linked her arm in his. "Let's go." She refrained from telling him how safe she felt while they walked arm-in-arm. If she did, he would argue with her about going to Terroria. Instead, she secretly welcomed the warmth and security that holding on to him offered, if only for a little while.

PICCOLO ITALIA DID not seem very busy for a Friday night. "Where is everyone?" Jackson asked.

Dante wiped his hands on his apron. "Been and gone. We close in fifteen minutes."

Jackson looked at the clock on the wall. "Do you believe it's already eleven fifteen?"

"Time flies when you're on trial," Johanna murmured.

"We can still get slices, can't we?" he asked.

"I've got three plain slices left and one mushroom."

"Ugh, I hate mushrooms." Jackson made a face.

"I'll eat the mushroom slice," Johanna offered.

"Okay." He turned to Dante. "We'll take them all. And a couple of colas."

Dante slipped the slices in the oven, while Johanna and Jackson slid into a red leatherette booth across from the counter.

"Anyway, I was thinking," Jackson started, "that once I tell—"

"Stop."

"What?"

"You're dangerous when you think."

"I'm going with you."

"You have school."

"I'll just tell Old Man Benson that you need me to go with you."

"To another world, where the beings have tentacles for arms and alien eyes? I don't think so."

"You can't go alone."

"I *will* go alone. And you *do* need to ask Mr. Benson for three days off from school, because you have to run the library while I'm gone."

"They should have sentenced me to hard labor on Terroria, instead of you. You were there because of me. Besides, I don't know how to run the library."

"Yes, you do. Nobody is asking you to do any bookbinding or to research special exhibitions while I'm gone. All you have to do is open the mail, save the bills for me, and process the requests to borrow books. The list of approved borrowers is on the computer. I'm sure you know where to find it, because you're the person who entered all that information. That's all you have to do for three days, besides answer the phone. Tell anyone asking for me that I was suddenly called out of town and that I'm expected back on Thursday. What could be easier?"

"I still think—"

"Pizza's up," Dante shouted.

"Get our food. Then tell me all about the project you and Logan have planned for this weekend."

THAT NIGHT, JOHANNA's dreams were peppered with nightmares about all the horrible things that could happen on Terroria. She slept fitfully, and it was after nine by the time she woke up. She checked her messages, prepared two book deliveries, and grabbed her camera before heading out.

When she arrived at Mrs. Caruthers's house, Jackson and Logan, along with what looked like half the neighborhood, were already busy scraping old paint off the siding and chopping up the broken sidewalk. Cassie walked around the house with a clipboard in hand, jotting down ideas for plants. Brittany and Chris painted new shutters, so they would be dry enough to handle when it came time to attach them to the windows.

Johanna walked over to Jackson's mom, who stood with Ava in their adjoining yard. "So what does Mrs. Caruthers think of all this?"

"She doesn't know. Jackson made a deal with someone over at the senior center to get her out of the house. She's apparently a gifted quilter. They asked her to give a class in quilt making and offered to pay her fifty dollars, so she happily agreed."

"That's pretty amazing. Where did the money come from?"

"It's from a senior-center program. They have a grant that pays experts to teach classes. I hope it goes well."

"Me, too. I'd better start shooting video. I promised Jackson I'd edit it to music so he could post it online."

Mrs. Roth sniffed back a tear. "They're really something, these kids. They did the same thing for me last year, and I was overwhelmed. I'm so proud of them. But don't let me keep you. Go take pictures."

It turned out to be a long day, but Ava supplied everyone with lemonade and water, and the Students for a Better Society club at the high school brought sandwiches and brownies for the crew. It turned into more of a celebration than anything else, and the camaraderie made everyone work a little harder.

BY LATE AFTERNOON, Chris and Jackson had finished attaching the shutters to the house, and stood back to admire their work. The only thing they had overlooked was how long it would take the new concrete sidewalk in the front yard to dry.

"I hope Mrs. Caruthers has a key to the back door," Chris said. "I'd hate to have to break a windowpane to get her inside her fixed-up house."

The crowd cheered when the senior-transit van pulled up in front of the house. Everyone waited anxiously for Mrs. Caruthers to get out of the vehicle, but after a very long interval, only the driver emerged.

"Is everything all right?" Mrs. Roth asked.

"She's crying. She wanted to know why all these people are standing in front of her house, and when I told her, she became very emotional. She needs a moment to compose herself."

Slowly, Mrs. Caruthers climbed out of the vehicle, her eyes bright with tears. Mrs. Roth pulled a tissue out of her pocket and offered it to the elderly woman.

"Thank you, dear." Mrs. Caruthers sighed deeply and made her way toward the front door.

Jackson reached for her arm. "I'm sorry, Mrs. Caruthers, you can't go in that way, for now. The cement is still wet. Do you have a key to the back?"

She nodded, and then her head movement changed from up and down to side to side. "Why ...?" She could not finish her thought.

Jackson turned on the charm. "You know, you're a pillar of this community." He slipped his arm around her shoulders. "And you've always watched out for us. This is just a gesture from your friends and neighbors that we're watching out for you, too, and we're here to help you. If you need help ..."

A giant tear rolled down the old woman's cheek. "Thank you, Jackson. This is the nicest thing anyone has ever done for me."

"Let me introduce you to everyone who helped

out." Jackson called out each volunteer by name. He told her about every person's contribution to the project, and Mrs. Caruthers shook hands with each and every one of them, to thank them personally.

Johanna captured it all on video, glad that her tears did not splash onto the camera lens and blur the images.

JOHANNA STAYED OUT late with Jackson and his friends, celebrating the success of their community project, but in the back of her mind, she couldn't shake the fact that her sentence would begin in forty-eight hours.

It was after two in the morning when she finally crawled into bed. She yawned with exhaustion, but her looming incarceration prevented her from getting much sleep. Finally, she gave into her insomnia, brewed a pot of coffee, and grabbed Mal's diary.

"Mal, why were you on Terroria?"

She waited. After several minutes passed with no word from her mentor, she felt abandoned. Then, the pages riffled to a section near the end. The diary outlined how Mal had been summoned to appear before the Library of Illumination's College of Overseers to testify on behalf of Johanna, who had admitted to destroying Terrorian property. According to his diary entry:

> I had initially thought the punishment too harsh, but then I discerned an undercurrent of deep concern among the overseers. It began when I testified about reports that I had heard about obelisks being counterfeited so the originals could be sold to finance weaponry. The overseers dismissed me, but more importantly, they did not dispute my testimony. I am

*sure the College of Overseers needs Johanna
to serve her sentence on Terroria, so that she
can act as its eyes and ears on that world. I am
quite certain she is being planted as a spy.*

Johanna gasped when she read Mal's words. *Counterfeits. Weapons. Spy.* She would have to keep her eyes and ears open for any indication of warmongering and subterfuge. Well, maybe not her ears, not unless the overseers reinstated her ability to understand the Terrorians. *They'll have to, or else how am I supposed to know what Nero 51 expects of me?*

Three days. She planned to travel light. Nothing fancy—just a change of clothes, a toothbrush, and protein bars in a backpack. And water. She would need to bring her own water. She didn't even know if they *had* water on Terroria. She spent the rest of the day trying to find out as much as she could about the realm. She didn't expect it to be easy, but when she plugged Terroria into the library database, listings for it came right up. Finding them would be another matter. They were located on sub-level fifty-six. *Could that be in the basement?*

She picked up Mal's diary and consulted it again. "Where's sub-level fifty-six?"

The diary opened to a section she had never seen before. It contained page after page of detailed floor plans, starting with the cupola and ending with sub-level 1,311. The plans for most of the sub-levels looked the same. They were made up of countless rows of stacks filled with every book, pamphlet, drawing, musical composition, letter, treaty, mathematical equation, and other tangible collection of words, numbers, symbols and ideas the realms had ever known.

"How do I get down to sub-level fifty-six?"

The pages shuffled again, and a picture of an archaic hand-crank elevator appeared. *Hand crank—for fifty-six levels? Going down might not be so bad, but coming back up would be a bitch.*

"Mal, do you know if it's hard to crank?"

A new entry by Mal appeared.

The original apparatus has been upgraded many times. The container was last replaced in the mid–nineteenth century with an open cage elevator that may look old but is in good working order. It is easy to operate. The hand crank has also been replaced, and the device is nuclear powered, just like everything else in the library.

Johanna breathed a sigh of relief.

"Are you okay?"

She jumped. She hadn't heard Jackson come in the back door. "I'm fine. I located books on Terroria on sub-level fifty-six."

"Where?"

"My thought exactly. If you come with me, we can find it together."

She led him down into the basement to the area where Mal's diary had indicated the existence of an elevator. A large shelf cabinet containing library castoffs stood where the elevator should be. An old adding machine, a broken postage meter, and other obsolete office equipment that had seen better days filled the shelves.

"Look for a lever," she said.

They inspected every shelf, removing the junk and piling it on the floor so they could spot the lever more easily.

"I don't see any," Jackson observed, while pressing on the backs of the shelves, looking for a way to get them to swing open.

"It's too dark in here." The absence of windows made it hard to see in shadowy corners. "See if that light still works."

Jackson inspected a tarnished brass frame encasing an old-fashioned light bulb. "I don't see any switch. Maybe I just need to tighten the bulb ... if I can get my fingers through these stupid bars." The frame made reaching the bulb difficult. "I wonder if this thing comes off," he said, twisting it. As he did so, the shelf slid open, sending up a cloud of dust.

"You're like an accidental genius," Johanna said, with a smile.

"Thanks ... I think."

Hidden behind the shelf was an ancient cage made of brass bars. It had a bronze medallion affixed to the front of it: *LOI*. Johanna pulled the door open and pushed aside an inner scissor-gate. She tentatively entered the elevator, and Jackson followed. They looked at the massive panel of numbers. The number *6* was already lit. The button for the lowest level said *1311*. She found the button for sub-level fifty-six and pushed it. The elevator lurched as it started its descent.

—LOI—

LOI

CHAPTER FIVE

JOHANNA DIDN'T KNOW what to expect on sub-level fifty-six, but envisioned something dark, dirty, and in disrepair. Instead she found a comfortable space filled with abundant soft lighting and climate-controlled air. She located the section where the computer catalog system said she would find books on Terroria, and she soon chose one that looked promising.

"That was easy," Jackson said, as they headed back to the elevator.

"All things considered," she agreed, "we got off lucky."

They hopped on the elevator, and Jackson studied the buttons. "What floor? I've never seen an elevator in the library. Do you think there's a door hidden behind one of the shelves?"

"I'm pretty sure the basement is level six. Press that button. We can look for an elevator on the main floor after this is all over."

The cage made a creaking sound as it started to ascend. Jackson gazed at the staircase that wound around the elevator as it climbed. "Could you imagine if we had to walk up all these stairs to get back? There must be thousands of them. Tens of thousands, if the library really does go down to"—he inspected the button panel—"sub-level thirteen-hundred and eleven."

The cage suddenly stopped between floors, and the lights went out.

"No, no, no, no, no." Johanna huffed.

The lights suddenly turned on, and the elevator began moving again.

"Frit. My heart dropped to my stomach when that happened. I wouldn't want to be stuck down here. No one would even know where we were. We would starve to death. Maybe even have to kill one another for food." He thought about that for a second. "Don't worry, I could never do that to you. You could eat me first."

"Uh-huh." She left it at that.

"You're supposed to say that you would do the same thing for me."

"It grieves me to say that you would have to die alone, because the College of Overseers is coming tomorrow evening to escort me to my sentence, and I get the feeling that they would find me no matter where I am."

"That's probably true. You don't think they would leave me down there, do you?"

The elevator stopped. Johanna opened the scissor-gate and stepped out. "I guess we'll never know."

They sat together on the sofa. "Be prepared in case the Terrorians appear."

She opened the back cover and immediately

inspected the bottom of the endpaper. "It's a zero. We're safe."

"How do you know?"

"Mal's diary. I saw a section about how the library's collection has a hint about the book levels camouflaged in the endpapers." She turned the book and showed him a minute *0*.

"That could come in handy. When were you going to tell me?"

"I just read it this morning," she replied.

She paged through the *History of Terroria*. It gave details on Realm Twelve from its earliest days through the present, and included the curators who had overseen it. There was a section on Terrorians' major contributions to music, art, and literature, and a detailed geographical outline of the world and its natural resources. The book also touched upon the portals, and how all the libraries had full use of them for communicating with the other realms, until the Two Millennia War.

> *Terroria's impatience with some of the other realms, as well as its unbridled thirst for power, resulted in a scheme to take over the entire library system. The Terrorian Realm formed alliances with Adventura and Mysteriose to overturn the Council of Twelve (now defunct), a governing board formed by the curators of each of the realms. In a well-planned coup d'état, the three rogue curators seized control of the Council of Twelve and commanded their troops to use the portals to invade each library and take over its operation. The population of each realm resisted the invaders, but could not break the defenses of the well-protected libraries. The nine realms that*

refused to join with the Terrorians, Adventurites, and Mysterians suffered severe deprivation at the hands of their captors. The population on some worlds decreased by more than two-thirds.

The College of Overseers moved to seal the portals, isolating the rebels in nine separate battles. The overseers immediately convened the First Inter-Realm Peace Council. Rebel leaders agreed to attend, but as soon as the portals reopened, Terrorian curator Claff 8 ordered new troops to transport into the war zones and push for victory. He took two of the overseers prisoner and had them executed in a demonstration of power.

The remaining overseers escaped and sealed the portals again—scrambling their configuration so anyone breaching a portal would never be sure where he or she might emerge.

The war raged on until the overseers secretly built a one-way portal to a containment cell in Lumina. In a stunning use of reverse propaganda, the overseers leaked information that the portal doors would be opened so a secret emissary could travel between worlds, but in fact, no such visit had been planned. Instead, all the portals were reconfigured to lead only to the Luminan cell. In a stunning victory, all newly recruited rebel fighters, along with Claff 8, were captured. The Terrorian curator turned his weapon on himself, rather than become a prisoner. Many of the other fighters broke down and told the Luminans everything they knew about the military operation. Claff 8's allies were taken into custody and, after cross-examination, *found guilty of treason and put to death.*

Special Luminan troops traveled to each realm to restore order. A substantial amount of blood continued to be shed during the following half century, while Lumina battled to regain control of all the Libraries of Illumination. Once peace was established, new curators who swore loyalty to the College of Overseers were put into place, and the portals sealed. The Two Millennia War had ended, but would never be forgotten, especially by those realms that suffered the deepest losses. (For more information, refer to "The New Epoch" by Summeria 15.)

"Do you think the Terrorians still hold a bit of a grudge against the overseers?" Jackson asked.

"It's possible, although that was a very long time ago."

"Nero 51's living room had piles of stuff that looked like rocket launchers. They were huge."

"Did he say anything when he put you behind the force field?"

"Ik, ik, glug."

"Helpful."

"You asked."

"Mal is pretty sure they're counterfeiting obelisks to buy weapons, which would give credence to your observation of a stockpile of heavy artillery. Did you get a peek into any of the other rooms of the residence?"

"No. He slammed me inside that force field pretty quickly. And a moment later, you began banging on the door. Except, now that I think of it, I did see something that looked like a TV screen on the wall that he momentarily 'ik, ik, glugged' into. It may be some sort of communications device."

"I wonder if there's a book downstairs on the Terrorian language."

"Why? Are you planning to say 'how do you do' in Terrorian?"

"I'd like to know how they say words like *weapons, war, counterfeit,* and *invasion,* so that I'll know if they're talking about something other than literature."

"Well, if you're going to use the elevator, I'm going to stay behind. And if you're not back within a half-hour, I'll lasso the hook in *our* cupola and dial up the College of Overseers."

"Maybe I'd better take a flashlight and Mal's diary with me."

"You think Mal has a better chance of helping you than I do?"

"No. But I think he's an excellent backup plan."

Johanna checked the computer for a book on Terrorian language and syntax, and found one listed on sublevel fifty-six. "Fifty-six must be the Terrorian level."

She grabbed what she needed, and Jackson followed her down to the basement and watched as she twisted the light fixture.

"The way I figure it," Jackson reasoned "it should only take you one minute to get down there, three minutes to find the book, and another minute to get back up. After that, I'm calling in the troops."

"You gave me a half-hour just a few minutes ago."

"Just hurry."

Johanna entered the elevator. Before she could slide the scissor-gate shut, the lights blinked.

"See what I mean?" Jackson added.

"I'll be back before you know it."

* * *

A REALM AWAY, a society of select Terrorians met in secret. One member of the group, Zor 114, discussed how they might be able to hack into the portals and take control of their operation. He attempted a demonstration, but after a promising flash, it failed.

During those attempts, the power on twelve different worlds ... blinked.

JOHANNA FOUND THE language primer quickly and hurried back up to sub-level six. Jackson awaited her there, as promised.

"Four minutes. Not bad. Let's go back upstairs. For some reason, this place is giving me the creeps."

Johanna cracked open the book, thankful for another Level Zero designation. Jackson sat down next to her and read aloud from the middle of the page. "Ik, ock, uk: *I am; you are; he, she, or it is.* What are all these funny symbols?"

"The conjugation of ik, ock, uk, written in Terrorian."

"While you were down there, you should have looked for a Terrorian-English dictionary."

"Yeah. Why don't you just go download one on the iPad while I study this."

"Good one." He sat back and closed his eyes.

Johanna turned to the back of the book to see if a word list or glossary existed. She found what she wanted and looked up *weapons*. "Ergat."

"You gargling?"

"I'm saying the word for *weapon*. Ergat."

"That's an easy one. Wyatt Earp carried a gun. Mobsters called a gun a gat. 'Er' for Earp, 'gat' for gun."

She marveled at Jackson's ability to make anything sound simple. "Cru."

"What's that?"

"*War.*"

"Okay, war is cruel. Just cut off the end. What's it say for 'counterfeit'?"

"Nothing. There's no listing in here for fake, phony, or even bogus."

"There's got to be some equivalent."

"Noh."

"There has to be."

"I didn't say 'no'—n-o—I said 'noh'—n-o-h—which means 'copy' or 'reproduction.'"

"Oh. That's a 'noh'-brainer."

She sighed, even though the corners of her mouth turned up just a little. "Guz."

"Does that mean they're going to cut out your gizzard and guzzle your blood?"

"Close. It means 'invade.'"

"What's the future tense of 'ik, ock, uk'?"

Johanna turned back the pages. "Iki, ocko, uku, ikin, ockon, ukin."

"Rhymes with ..."

"Stop it."

"Okay. If you hear someone say, 'Ikin guz,' it means we will invade."

"Porg."

"We will invade pork?"

"Porg means 'portal.'"

"How do you say 'takeover'?"

She turned the pages. "There's nothing listed for 'takeover,' but there is 'seg.'"

"What does that mean?"

"'Seize.' So if I hear anyone say, 'Ikin seg porg,' I'll know they're planning to seize the portals."

As Johanna tried to commit words to memory,

Jackson made up little mnemonic devices to help her absorb them. She laughed at his attempts because they sounded goofy, but had to admit they actually helped her learn Terrorian.

"Do you know this one?" he asked. "Bli z' Bril."

"Cold?"

He smiled. "If you're talking about your answer, it *is* cold. 'Bli z' Bril' means 'Library of Illumination' in Terrorian."

WHEN THE CLOCK struck nine, Johanna kicked Jackson out. "Go home. You've got school tomorrow, and I've got to rest up so I can spend the day learning about Terroria and tying up loose ends here at the library."

"I'm thinking of taking tomorrow off."

"Don't. I need the time to get stuff done."

"I can help you."

"You can help me after school. We didn't get back here until around eleven on Friday night, so they won't be coming for me until late tomorrow. If you come straight after school, we'll have plenty of time to go over everything you'll need to do here while I'm away."

He made a face at her.

She pulled him over and kissed him. "Really, it's going to be all right."

"I hope so."

NORMALLY, JOHANNA DIDN'T mind Monday mornings, but this one filled her with anxiety. She dressed quickly and made herself a huge breakfast. She would be taking protein bars to Terroria to help her keep up her energy, but she wanted to make sure that she ate several hearty meals before leaving Exeter. Earth. Fantasia. Realm Eleven. *Whew.* Everything she had learned in the past seventy-two hours boggled her mind.

She crammed everything she thought she'd need in her backpack, and placed it by the circulation desk. She packed Mal's diary, but then unpacked it to ask a question.

"Mal, if I leave Jackson my diary, will he be able to read it the way I can read yours, and ask questions?"

His words crawled across the page: *A curator has the ability to read the diary of either a mentor or a protégé.*

She grabbed her diary and quickly scanned it. Mal had given it to her when she became his protégé. She placed it on the circulation desk.

"How will I know if Jackson asks a question? Will I be able to see it?"

You will sense it. And once you consciously think of the answer, it will appear in your diary. It will be a mostly one-way conversation, however, because Jackson will have no way of knowing if you are trying to reach him.

"Thanks, Mal." She closed his diary and slipped it in her backpack. She kept busy for the rest of the day by doing chores around the library and memorizing as much Terrorian language and lore as possible.

"How's it going?"

She jumped when she heard Jackson's voice. "Is it that late already?"

"I had to ask Old Man ... uh ... Mr. Benson for the next few days off to take care of the library, and I asked if I could leave an hour early so you could *mentor* me. He's so happy about all the positive feedback he's getting about our community-service project that he was happy to oblige. It's like being a superstar. I can get anything I want right now."

"Help me with my Terrorian. Even better, sit

down, relax, and think back to when Nero 51 grabbed you. I need you to tell me everything. What you saw, what you felt, what you smelled, what you heard."

"I thought we already went over all that?"

"You said he spoke to someone. Can you recall what he said?"

"I'll need to close my eyes for this."

Jackson sat on the sofa and put his head back. He envisioned the tentacles pulling him into the residence. He recalled the acrid, metallic smell—like a chemical lab—and while most of the Terrorian library was merely hazy, he remembered the residence contained an oily mist rising from the floor.

"It smelled really bad, like a solvent mixed with rotten eggs. I could actually taste it when I inhaled, but then he picked up a weapon and shot me, and I didn't really think about it after that."

"You didn't tell me he shot you."

"He didn't shoot me with bullets or arrows or anything like that. He shot me with a force field that locked me in place."

"What did the weapon look like?"

"Like all the other weapons piled up against the wall."

"How many were there?"

"A hundred, maybe? Didn't you see them?"

"I was too focused on getting you out of there."

"Yeah, well, if we hadn't made a run for it before Nero 51 returned, he would have probably used the same weapon on you."

"So their weapons can immobilize any enemy without killing them?"

"Yeah."

"Which means they want them alive."

"Yeah."

"Why?"

"Dinner? Slavery? Maybe they want people to work the mines. Or maybe, they want to brainwash them and turn them into soldiers, so their own people don't get killed on the front lines."

"The front lines ..."

"Yeah. I think they're planning something big. I didn't know what 'cru' meant at the time, but I'm sure Nero 51 said it to the communication device."

"Did he use the word *tec*?"

"Maybe. I don't remember. What does it mean?"

"'Spy.'"

"Did you learn anything touristy, like 'I'm thirsty' or 'where is the bathroom'?"

"No." She looked them up. "There is no word for 'thirsty.' Apparently Terrorians absorb liquid from the air." She thumbed through the book for several minutes while Jackson quietly looked on. "Ewww. They don't have bathrooms, either. That thick, hazy vapor is their 'waste product,' which is discarded through their feet. We walked through that stuff."

"Everyone walked through that stuff, including the overseers."

"This is going to be the longest three days of my life."

"You'd better pack a roll of toilet paper."

Johanna slumped back against the cushions.

Jackson picked up her hand. "I'll be with you every step of the way. I won't stop thinking about you until you return."

"Oh." She jumped off the sofa to fetch her diary. She handed it to him. "This is my diary. It has a lot in it about how things work in the library. If you're stuck and need to ask me a question, write it in the diary on the last page. I'll sense it and can tell you the answer if I know it. Check it often, even just to ask how I'm doing, so I can answer you, or else there's no way I can stay in touch with you."

"What about Mal's diary?"

"I'm taking it with me."

"What if they take it from you?"

Her eyes widened with alarm. "Do you think they'll do that?"

"If they think it's important to you, they might. If they think they can get secret information about our library, they might."

"I never thought of that. Maybe I should leave it here."

"Why don't you ask Mal?"

WHEN JOHANNA POSED the question, Mal did not reply, but she felt the diary shrinking in her hand. It finally stopped when it was a half inch wide and three-quarters of an inch long. A small, metal loop grew out of one corner, and a little glass peephole appeared in the front. She raised it to her eye and saw her last entry. "Mal, do you hear me?"

She peeked inside and saw the word *Yes*.

"I'll be right back." She practically flew up the stairs and went straight to her jewelry box. She returned with a gold chain that she attached to the book and then placed around her neck, slipping the tiny tome under her tee shirt. She smiled at Jackson. "I feel better, now."

He picked up Johanna's diary and slipped it in his back pocket. "Don't worry about me. I don't need a shrinking diary. I'll just carry you around au naturel."

The clock struck eight. And Johanna's stomach

rumbled. "Pizza?"

"Okay. Relax. I'll run out and get it. You're getting a little jumpy."

"I'll call it in" she said, picking up her cell phone. As soon as Jackson left, she stuck the phone in her pocket. She sat on the sofa and closed her eyes.

Ω *This is no time to sleep, Johanna Charette. Your sentence has begun.*

—LOI—

LOI

A MOMENT LATER, Johanna and Overseer Plato Indelicat stood in front of the circulation desk on Terroria. Nero 51 was nowhere in sight. The overseer rang a large brass bell attached to the front of the desk.

"Uk infi," Nero 51 stated as he entered the area. The overseer waved his hand to enact a translation enchantment. *You're late.*

Ω *I have delivered Johanna Charette to you at the appointed hour. She is here to work off her sentence under the rules of the Arkan Peace Treaty, ratified after the Two Millennia War. She is to be treated in a civilized manner in accordance with her species, which is human. I will inspect her quarters, now.*

Nero 51 led the overseer to a small storage room toward the back of the library. It was empty except for the oily mist rising from the floor. The overseer waved his hand, and the mist vanished. A cot appeared, as well as a small sink and a toilet.

"You give preferences," Nero 51 practically shouted at him.

Ω *I am giving her the minimum accommodations necessary for her species.*

He turned to Johanna.

Ω *This room will serve you for one-third of every twenty-four hour period that you are here. You may spend seven consecutive hours here in repose, and one full hour dividing the workday for your meal break. You have merely to say the word 'sustenance,' and a meal made up of foods common to Fantasia will appear on this table.*

He waved his hand again, and a small table and a single chair appeared.

"You coddle the spy. Call me when she is ready to begin serving her sentence." Nero 51 left them alone.

Ω *As you can tell, I have enacted a translation enchantment, so that you can understand what Nero 51 and his minions expect of you. I will be back in seventy-two hours to escort you home. Be Illuminated, Johanna Charette.*

She dropped her backpack on the cot. The overseer disappeared, and Johanna found herself transported back to the front of the circulation desk. After waiting a moment, she rang the bell.

"You dare summon me."

"My sentence has begun."

A tentacle extended the width of the library to a utility closet and withdrew a rag and a jar of oily paste. "Polish the obelisks. If you dare to break one, you will be punished."

"I will need a ladder to reach the higher shelves."

"Find one," he snarled.

"I didn't want you to think I was snooping

around."

"Look in the utility closet."

"Thank you."

JOHANNA STARTED WITH the stacks to the right of the front door. She planned to work from top to bottom, but she wanted to determine what she was in for first. She selected an obelisk from a lower shelf. It was heavy, which she expected. The one that she had smashed had been just as heavy. As she opened the jar of paste, the noxious fumes nearly caused her to swoon. The odor resembled a cross between putrefied flesh and rotten fish, with a biting quality that stung her eyes and made them tear. She pulled her tee shirt up over her nose to filter the air, and did her best. The paste made the obelisks slippery, and she was afraid of dropping one, so when she climbed to the upper shelves, she tucked the obelisk inside her belt. She also learned a drop of polish went a long way, so she used as little as possible.

Johanna worked mindlessly, but the constant climbing to retrieve crystals made her back and knees ache. It didn't help that the Terrorian day started just when her day should have been ending. She had been at it for hours, and relief washed over her when she heard a voice out of nowhere say, Ω *Johanna Charette, you may take a one-hour meal break.*

She returned to her room and lay down on the cot. It turned out to be more comfortable than it looked. She thought back to Nero 51 accusing the overseer of coddling her, and wondered if it was true. It took a while before she felt her back muscles relax. She remained on the cot for a half-hour, then sat at the table and said, "Sustenance." A plate filled with carrots and peanuts appeared before her, as well as an old-fashioned tankard. She picked up the cup and sniffed. *Apple juice.* She consumed everything the overseers provided, and slipped a protein bar in her pocket.

Hardly a moment had passed when a voice said, Ω *Return to work.*

By the end of the day, she had polished most of the obelisks along the outer walls of the first story. It had been a massive effort, but hardly enough to make a small dent in the number of crystals in the building. She silently kept track of how many times she saw Nero 51. He spent a great deal of time in the antechamber and the residence, and she only saw him every couple of hours, when he would cross from one space to the other.

At the rate she was polishing obelisks, she would never reach the second level, or the curator's residence. She hoped to get a peek inside, or at least to eavesdrop on some snippet of conversation, but she may as well have been on an iceberg off the coast of Siberia, for all the good her proximity to the Terrorian war effort was doing.

BACK ON FANTASIA—as Jackson now liked to call it— sudden demands on his workload kept him on his toes. It started when the president of the library's board of directors called and demanded to speak to Johanna.

"She's out of town," Jackson explained.

"What do you mean, 'out of town'? We have no record of a request for time off."

"Her grandmother ... is dying," the teen fudged.

"Oh. Well. Who's taking her place?"

"I am, sir."

"And who are you?"

"Jackson Roth, Johanna's assistant." He paused. "You must know about me. I'm her curator-in-training. Just ask any of the overseers of the Library of Illumination

... uh ... foundation."

"Aren't you just a kid?"

"I'm the curator-in-training."

"Well, *Mr. Curator-In-Training*, some of the libraries in our neighboring communities are impressed with our facility's new information retrieval system. I've invited about two dozen of them to view a live demonstration of it on Thursday evening."

"No," Jackson said.

"Yes," the president of the board of directors stated emphatically. "I'm sure you can find money in your budget for some coffee and cookies. If we play our cards right, we could be named 'Library of the Year.' It's an honor that I would hate to see snatched away from us by a less prestigious facility that's still operating in the dark ages. We would be forced to *cut jobs* if that were to happen, if you get my drift."

"Right. A demonstration for a couple dozen people, with snacks, on Thursday evening," Jackson confirmed.

"At seven."

"Gotcha."

Click.

How hard can it be? He had helped Johanna set up evenings like this before. Clear out the furniture, set up some chairs, call the gourmet food shop in the village for coffee and cookies. *Easy peasy.*

He thought about the demonstration. How would he show all those people how easily the system worked? A large-screen TV would allow him to illustrate his workflow.

He called the president of the board of directors back.

"What is it?" The man sounded a little snarky.

"This is Jackson Roth, the curator-in-training at the Library of Illumination. There's the matter of a large-screen TV. I need one to stream our new digitized system, so your guests can see how well it works. Unfortunately, the library board rejected our request last fall. I'm so sorry, but that oversight will prevent me from demonstrating the system."

"What?"

"No TV, no ability to live stream my digital demonstration."

"That is not an option. Order the damn TV."

"Plus installation, of course."

"Just do it."

Jackson smiled. *This management stuff is easy.* He called The Guys Next Door—an appliance store in the village—and explained what he needed.

"What's the P.O. number?"

"We don't have a P.O. box. I'll give you the street address."

"Not post office—*purchase order*. What's the purchase-order number?"

"I'll have to get back to you." Jackson put down the phone and began to pace. It helped him think. Unfortunately, he lacked the experience or knowledge necessary to continue. *Johanna's diary.* It was right there in his back pocket. He dredged up a memory of her using it to contact Mal. He wrote down the words as he said them. "Johanna, how to you get a P.O. number?" *It stands for purchase order,* he added, just in case she was confused.

JOHANNA HEARD JACKSON'S voice in her head.

She said aloud, "Why do you need a purchase order?"

After a minute she heard Jackson reply, "The president of the library board told me to get a TV for a demonstration that he's scheduled here. The Guys Next Door asked for a P.O. number."

"There's a pad in the top right drawer of my desk that says 'purchase order' on it. They're pre-numbered. Fill out the next blank page. Take the top copy to the president of the library board for his signature, then give it to The Guys Next Door."

"Thanks," she heard him say. "How are you doing?"

"It's okay. The overseers are making sure I'm treated humanely."

"Anything you need?"

"Diet Coke with ice."

"Right."

Her evening meal seemed astonishingly similar to chicken soup—at least, she hoped it was made out of chicken. It contained meat and a variety of vegetables, accompanied by something that looked like bread that had been run over by a truck. Surprisingly, her tankard held beer. She had never been much of a beer drinker, but after the day she had endured, it quenched her thirst.

She lay down on the cot to contemplate her next move, and felt something poking her—her cell phone. She switched it off and stuck it in her backpack. She would have no use for it here. The next thing she knew, the voice in her head warned her that her workday would begin in twenty minutes.

DAY TWO SEEMED tediously comparable to day one. After her midday break, Johanna saw Nero 51 go up to the second floor, followed by several other Terrorians. *I believe I'll continue polishing obelisks on the outer walls before working my way in to the interior stacks. Since I'm done down here ...*

She climbed up to the next level and began working on the crystals that lined the shelves next to the residence. She couldn't hear a word they said, which was really disappointing. *Maybe when they're done.* With luck, they would continue their conversation as they exited the apartment, and she would learn something of value.

Johanna's stomach growled. She pulled a protein bar from her pocket, but before she could remove the packaging, the door to the residence slid open. She shoved the bar behind the obelisks and grabbed a rag, polishing the closest crystal.

NERO 51 FUMED when he saw Johanna near his residence. *This Fantasian is nothing but trouble.* He wished he could delay his meeting until after she left, but the very fact she was on Terroria was the only thing keeping the portals from being sealed. *We must be ready by tomorrow.* He cursed the overseers for putting a translation enchantment on his library. He would have to contact his followers and demand a night meeting at an outside location. They must prepare. He would be forced to leave the girl alone on the premises; however, anything she learned would not matter once they claimed victory.

He waited until she retreated to her room for the evening. Once he heard her door latch in to place—a precaution taken by the overseers—he walked to the front entrance and hit a switch on a control panel. Giant fans that blew warm, humid air into the library stopped running. *No use wasting precious humidity on the Fantasian.*

JOHANNA'S SUSTENANCE CONSISTED of a fish cake and

a hill of beans. *Edamame.* She thought of the protein bar that she had left on one of the shelves outside the residence. She held her breath as she opened her door, praying Nero 51 was not out inspecting her work. She popped her head out just in time to see him disappear out the front door.

Something struck her as odd. The mechanical sound that droned day and night suddenly stopped. She wondered what it meant.

Nero 51 entered Building 7, a neighboring structure at the end of the block. Almost everyone he contacted had already assembled there. "Where is Heil 66?"

"Printing maps of the realms. They must be ready by morning."

Nero 51 nodded. "Before dusk tomorrow, our teams should be ready to amass outside each portal. They must be indistinguishable from the library patrons I have invited to a special fundraising event in the cupola. There should be no reason to question anyone being there."

The gathering had originally been organized as a bona fide meeting, and it proved to be fortuitous planning after the teenagers from Realm Eleven breached the portals. Nero 51 decided at the outset that the Fantasians were too young and stupid to be spies. His accusations were deliberately intended to keep the portals open, until Terrorians could use them to invade the other libraries. He knew the overseers would impart *justice.*

"You could not have planned better," Opel 29 stated. "If we had dialed the overseers as originally planned, they may have suspected our motives. Instead, we are reacting to an external intrusion, and the element of surprise will be ours."

Operation Final Darkness would begin in less

than twenty-four hours.

THE LEVER TO the residence was missing, just like when she had tried to rescue Jackson. She crossed her fingers. "Illumination." Nothing happened.

She took a deep breath. "Delumination." The door remained sealed.

She had never been within hearing distance when Nero 51 entered his apartment, yet something poked the back of her brain. For some reason, she conjured up an image of Jackson grinning. *What did he say?* She closed her eyes for a moment and scanned her memory for something he had said, which she should have known, but didn't.

Ahhh ... "Bli z' Bril."

The door vibrated as it slid out of the way. She tentatively entered the residence. The thick, oily mist inside the private quarters made her gag. She remembered what she had read about it and hated having to wade through it. A light would have been helpful, but she dared not use one, for fear of being caught. The building across the courtyard was lit, and let in just enough of a glow to illuminate the cache of weapons stacked against the wall. She did a quick count and moved into the next room. It also appeared to be filled with weapons, although it was difficult to tell because they obscured the window, eliminating it as a potential light source. The only reason why she could see at all was because the entry door remained open and the library proper was still illuminated.

She returned to the living room and looked for a desk. She found a short column shrouded in the haze that held several obelisks. It did not appear to have any drawers, and while she had taken the time to learn some Terrorian words, she had not learned the symbols that went with them, so she could not read the obelisks.

The room dimmed. Johanna glanced through the window and noticed the light from the other building had gone out. There was nothing more she could learn here. She slipped out the door, but it did not automatically close. "Bli z' Bril," she said aloud. As the residence door whooshed shut, the main door to the Library of Illumination creaked open. Nero 51 had returned, and Johanna stood immobilized—trapped—on the residence floor.

The Terrorian passed beneath her on his way to the curator's staircase. Johanna slipped to the front shelf that separated the apartment from the balcony overlooking the main reading room. If this library was a duplicate of her own, she'd find a tiny space between the end shelf and a front window. She scurried to it, pressed herself into the space, and held her breath.

"Bli z' Bril." *Swoosh.*

She waited for a second swoosh that would tell her the door had closed. She heard the latch snap into place, and quietly released her breath. *I just need to get to the staircase.* She waited a minute before stealthily sneaking to the spiral stairs. She had not paid attention to whether they squeaked, and prayed with each step she took. Downstairs, she hurried back to her room and heard the door latch loudly click into place. She wondered if Nero 51 heard it as well.

Johanna picked up Mal's diary. "What should I do if I found several rooms filled with weapons?" she whispered. She held the tiny book up to her eye and waited. After several minutes, a single line of type appeared.

Nothing. You are only there to serve out your sentence.

Johanna's face wrinkled. She thought the overseers wanted her to learn as much as she could about the Terrorian plot, but now Mal stated that she must merely serve her sentence. She slumped. *Did Mata Hari have to go through this?*

JACKSON ROLLED HIS shoulders. Even with the help of the dumbwaiter, removing enchanted books from the most accessible stacks turned out to be a back breaker. He had worked well into the evening, and had conked out on the sofa in the main reading room.

He spent most of the following morning re-populating the shelves with the old unenchanted books they had stored in the basement. *Good thing we never sold these back to Bebe's Bibliothèque.* He was almost done when he heard someone banging on the front door.

"Are you from The Guys Next Door?" It was a dumb question. Their uniforms had the company name emblazoned across them, and they stood next to a huge box decorated with a full-size picture of a sixty-inch flat-screen TV.

"Yeah. Where do you want it?"

Jackson surveyed the library. In the back of his mind, he had always thought it would be cool to have a TV rise out of the back of the circulation desk, but that would require special cabinetry. And a budget (he had learned about the importance of budgeting when he opened the petty-cash box the day before and found only $11.45 for coffee and cookies. The bill was actually four times that amount, and he ended up paying the difference with his own money). Regardless, the circulation desk seemed like the most logical place for a TV. "Put it here, facing those chairs."

"You got an antenna or cable hookup back here?"

It was another one of those questions he didn't know the answer to. "You go ahead and unpack it while I find out." He consulted Johanna's diary in the antechamber. He didn't want the repairmen to think he was some kind of nut when he asked it a question.

OUTSIDE THE TERRORIAN library, Heil 66 lumbered along, hidden in the shadows of the building across the way. He had been delayed making maps for the war effort, and needed to leave them for the troops gathering in Building 7. He saw Nero 51 reenter the library and knew he had missed that night's meeting. Seconds later, he saw a fleeting shadow in a second-floor library window. Nero 51 was strong, but not necessarily quick. Heil 66 doubted his compatriot could have reached the upper level so swiftly. He watched, waiting. The shadow appeared a second time, several minutes after the first darkening. The mapmaker waited to see if anyone would emerge from the Library of Illumination. Anyone trying to escape the building would have to use the front door, because the rear entrance had been sealed shortly after the start of the Two Millennia War and had never been reopened. The night was raw, and Heil 66 wrapped his unoccupied tentacles around his body to keep his moist emissions from evaporating.

An hour elapsed. There had been no further shadows nor disturbances of any kind, so the Terrorian continued on his journey. *It's probably nothing.* Still, as he hurried along to Building 7, he made a mental note to mention the shadows to Nero 51.

LOI

CHAPTER SEVEN

JOHANNA SAT AT the edge of her cot staring into space. Jackson's voice broke the silence. "Do we have a cable hookup or TV antenna near the circulation desk?"

She had no idea, but she knew where to find the information. She asked Mal's diary. She waited several minutes for an answer.

No need. Any device inside the library will wirelessly absorb any transmission signals. Just plug it in and let it warm it up. No further setup is required.

She relayed the message to Jackson, wondering what she would find when she returned to the library. *My library.*

That night, Johanna slept restlessly. Her only solace was that at the end of her sentence, she could burrow beneath the blankets of her own bed.

Finally she fell asleep, but could not escape her dreams.

She worked feverishly in the cupola of the Terrorian library, trying to clean obelisks. Every time she reached for one, it floated away. Nero 51 had ordered her to clean them all, or she would not be allowed to leave the Twelfth Realm. With her future at stake, Johanna chased the crystals around the cupola, trying to grab them, but as soon as she wrapped her fingers around one, it fell to the floor and shattered.

She panicked, sweat oozing from her pores. She tried picking up the broken pieces, but could barely see them through the hazy mist. Perspiration made her hands slippery, and the shards she found slipped through her fingers, cutting her hands and making them bleed. She managed to push the pieces off into a misty corner where she hoped they would not be discovered. She reached for another obelisk, but again, it eluded her. Try as she might, she could not grab on to it.

"Did I hear an obelisk break?" roared Nero 51.

She was so startled by his sudden appearance, her arm hit the shelf, and several of the crystal manuscripts crashed to the floor.

"She is willfully destroying library property," he shouted. "Off with her head."

Two other Terrorians appeared behind him, their tentacles snaking toward Johanna, to take her into custody. She tried to grab an obelisk to hurl at her captors, but the crystals continued to evade her grasp. Finally, she snatched one out of the air and hurled it at one of the Terrorians, but it bounced off his chest and dropped to the floor, where it bounced again, but didn't break. Amazement overcame her. Instead of continuing her attack, she dove for the unbroken obelisk. It was fashioned out of a plastic-like material that looked like the crystal obelisks but was indestructible. "Counterfeits," she screamed. "Fakes. Noh-nohs."

"Kill her now!"

Johanna felt a tentacle wrap around her throat. Another held her wrists while a third bound her feet. She gagged.

Ω*THE WORKDAY WILL begin in twenty minutes.*

Johanna's eyes flew open. She reached for her throat. The chain attached to Mal's diary had tangled around her neck. She pulled it loose, got out of bed, and splashed water on her face. *It was a dream.* She dropped down onto the chair. "Sustenance." A bowl of cold gruel and an apple appeared. The gruel had no taste, but it filled her stomach and stopped it from growling. The apple, at least, had flavor. She also received a tankard of weak tea, but no honey or sugar to sweeten it. She drank it to quench her thirst, knowing she had only one bottle of water left.

The dream haunted her. She thought of the obelisk that would not break. If the Terrorians had counterfeits, where would they be? Not on a shelf where anyone could find them. More than likely, they would be on a shelf that no one looked at. *The Cupola?* True, it was a seldom-used area of the library, but it meant carrying heavy obelisks up five flights of stairs. The least likely place would be among the main-floor stacks, the ones closest to the back wall, by the antiquities.

She berated herself for being so predictable. The obelisks she had polished were the most visible ones. Maybe today she would pick up a clue by investigating the ones buried in the stacks.

She exited her room. Nero 51 stood at the circulation desk, placing glass microscope slides into a box. *That can't be right.* They looked like microscope slides, but Johanna had a hunch they were documents of some sort.

She went to the utility closet and grabbed a rag and the jar of oily paste. She could feel Nero 51's eyes boring into the back of her head as she walked to an interior shelf and started polishing.

THE CURATOR SLIPPED the last bit of glass into a padded box. Time was of the essence, and he could not stop to bother about the girl, even though she was a nuisance. *Let her clean obelisks. She's not going to find anything. Even if she does, it's too late.*

He picked up the box and walked out the front door, switching off the humidity fans as he passed by. Terrorian soldiers awaited the information he carried—detailing the different realms, their curators, and the conditions rebel troops might face on each world. They had less than twenty-four hours to review maps and other forms of intelligence and complete their war preparations.

Nero 51 had grown up learning about the Two Millennia War and dreaming about the part he could have played in it. He imagined winning the war and being proclaimed "Grand Guardian of all the Libraries," a master of twelve different worlds—thirteen if you counted Lumina, the home of the Board of Overseers. He desired ultimate rule, and he would not allow some insignificant human female from Fantasia to disrupt his plans. *Johanna Charette, curator of the Eleventh Realm, I will make sure you are taken alive. I want to watch you being tortured. Yours will be a slow, painful death that will give me great pleasure.*

JACKSON ENTERED JOHANNA'S apartment. He felt uncomfortable being in her residence without her. He had debated asking her diary where he could find a blanket and a pillow, but didn't want to write something that might distract her—in a bad way. He knew they had to be there. Casanova had used them.

He stopped in front of two closed doors. He'd seen them during his previous visits to her home. He selected the one on the left and entered her private sanctuary. A four-poster bed dominated the space, and the comforter that topped it looked so fluffy, Jackson knew if he lay down on it he would sink halfway to the floor in a cloud of goose down. He looked around the room. Additional closed doors beckoned him. He pulled one open and found an en suite bathroom with a huge built-in tub. Creamy-white pillar candles decorated the back ledge, and he imagined them flickering, their light reflecting on the polished marble walls and mirrored surfaces while Johanna soaked in a mountain of bubbles. *No blanket or pillow in here.*

He pulled open the second door. It contained an L-shaped walk-in closet filled with very few clothes. Johanna dressed nicely, but he knew she didn't splurge on clothing the way Cassie and Brittany did. He sniffed. Her closet smelled just like her—baby powder and roses.

He looked at an empty hanging rod. *If I ever move in with Johanna, there's plenty of space for my stuff,* he thought, then shook his head. *Talk about a pipe dream.*

He walked back into the hallway and opened the other door. It was a linen closet, and sitting on the upper shelf, right at eye-level, he found a blanket and pillow. In the back of his mind he knew they would be there, but if he had opened that door first, he would not have had an excuse to explore her bedroom. *Tour over.* He grabbed the linens and carried them downstairs.

Jackson stretched out on the sofa. All he had left to do was test the visual presentation he had created for the group of visiting librarians, but that could wait until morning. *I've got it all under control,* he thought, before rolling onto his side and falling asleep.

JOHANNA NOTICED THE sudden silence when Nero 51 exited the building.

She continued polishing obelisks, but soon realized if she wanted to find what she sought, it would make more sense to pick the crystals up and hope the fakes felt different. She calculated fifty or sixty obelisks on each shelf, and hundreds of shelves. Thousands, even. She also had to consider the private book rooms, antiquities, erotica, periodicals ... she rubbed her temples as she felt the beginnings of a headache. *What if they're on a sub-level?*

She heard the front door open. She dipped a rag in the wax and polished another obelisk.

"Nero 51, are you here?"

"I told you he wouldn't be here," a second voice said. "He's probably already at Building 7."

"Where's the Fantasian creature? Shouldn't she be here? I want to get a look at her. I hear she's hideous."

Johanna could hear the Terrorians flat feet slapping against the floor. She continued polishing.

"Oh. Here she is."

"What a pathetic little beast."

"I know. But she's the key to our victory. The portals wouldn't be open if she weren't here."

"Shhh!"

"She can't understand us. I doubt she can speak Terrorian."

"Just hold your tongue. Anyway, there's nothing for us here. Let's go meet the others."

Johanna focused on their words. *The portals are open because I'm here. And I'm the key to their victory.* When she heard the door open, she peeked around the edge of the stacks and watched them leave. She began grabbing obelisks at random, hoping to find one that would prove to be false. She wanted to be able to give the Board of Overseers the proof they needed. Unfortunately, the obelisks all looked alike, so she had to pay very close attention to make sure she made progress.

Ω Johanna Charette, you may take a one-hour meal break.

She finished the shelf she'd been working on and left her cleaning supplies there, so she would know where she left off. She needed sustenance, and she wanted to tell Mal what the Terrorians had said. She choked down dense, grainy bread with some kind of vegetable mash, and followed it with orange juice. *This cuisine will never earn a Michelin star.*

She detailed what she had heard in Mal's diary. "What should I do?"

She waited quite a while before a reply appeared.

Nothing. You are only there to serve out your sentence.

She gritted her teeth. Her jaw clenched so tightly it gave her a headache. *I should have brought aspirin.*

Johanna left her room and looked around the library. It didn't look like anyone was there. She grabbed the rag and paste and climbed up to the second level. She placed her ear against the door of the residence, listening for any sounds coming from within. She heard nothing, and quietly said, "Bli z' Bril." The door opened, and she ducked inside.

The light of day brightened the room, and she tried to estimate the number of weapons. They were piled everywhere. She grabbed one from an inconspicuous area and left, but froze outside the door to the residence, her mind racing. The quickest way to her room was down the curator's staircase, but if Nero 51 walked in, he would surely take those stairs. Her intuition told her to take the stone steps by the front door. They would provide more cover once she got there, and she could ditch the gun behind the steps if she heard anyone enter. Using them, however, would force her to run around the very visible second balcony to the opposite end of the library, and then past the circulation desk on the main floor. That would be too much time out in the open. The Terrorians would not think twice about killing her.

Stop wasting time. By now she could have run down the stairs and been safely back in her room.

She heard a noise in the outer vestibule. She sprinted down the spiral stairs with the weapon raised above her head so it would not bang against the handrail. As she reached the bottom step, the front door screeched open. *The "juvenile" stacks should shield me from view.* She prayed she wouldn't be seen darting past the gaps that allowed light to flow throughout the space.

When she got into her room, she threw the

weapon under her cot, sat down, and said, "Sustenance." A bowl filled with yogurt appeared, a ripe peach and a cup of coffee beside it. She bit a huge chunk out of the peach and felt its juice run down her chin as her heart pounded. She could hear it quite clearly, even if it wasn't as loud as the pounding on her door.

—LOI—

LOI

CHAPTER EIGHT

"COME IN," SHE called out, as she stuffed a spoon of yogurt in her mouth.

"You're supposed to be working." Nero 51's eyes darted around the room.

"If the overseers told me my break was over, I would have heard them." Even as she said it, she racked her brain trying to remember if the message might have been drowned out by her escapade.

Ω *Johanna Charette, your break period has ended.*

The announcement came as if on cue. She bit into the peach again before standing up. "I guess I'll save this for later."

"You will not," Nero 51 said, grabbing the uneaten food in a tentacle and stretching it out the door and across the main reading room to dump it in a trash bin. "Get to work."

Johanna glared at him, but did not defy him. He

took one last look around the room, which made her heart pound. Plato Indelicat had removed the mist that might prevent Nero 51 from seeing the weapon, yet he did not comment on it. She worried that he *had* seen it but failed to mention it because he wanted her to lapse into a false sense of security. She had no recourse but to get back to polishing obelisks.

The hairs on the back of her neck suddenly stood on end. She had left the cleaning tools upstairs by the ladder. If Nero 51 saw them, he would know she had been snooping near the residence. She disappeared behind a stack and wondered what her next move should be.

JACKSON SHOT OFF the sofa when the television turned itself on at sunrise. He stumbled and then realized where he was. He looked to see if he had rolled over on the remote control, but found it on the circulation desk where he'd left it the previous night. He shut off the TV and walked around the library to make sure everything was secure. The main level seemed fine, and the public portions of the other levels appeared to be clear. Up in the cupola, he inspected the portal window he and Johanna had used. It looked sealed, but how could it be if Johanna had to use it to return home? The notion that Nero 51 and his pals could come flying through it at any given moment made him shiver. *Thank God Johanna's coming home tonight and the portals will be sealed.*

His imagination shifted into overdrive. What if a few Terrorians slipped through with her when she returned and held them hostage? Would the College of Overseers even know if that happened? *They would have to know. One of them will probably escort Johanna home.* The Terrorians would have to take the overseer hostage as well, and then everyone would know what had happened, because it would mean the beginning of a revolutionary multi-world war.

Stop it. You're making yourself crazy. Although, craziness might explain his sudden desire to buy a gun—just in case.

"HAVE YOU LOST your mind? Who do you think is going to sell a gun to a seventeen-year-old?" Logan bellowed over the telephone.

"Lots of people our age get guns. I hear about them all the time."

"It's illegal."

"All right. Forget I ever mentioned it."

"No. I want to know why you need a gun."

"What part of 'just forget it' don't you understand?"

"All of it."

"I've got to get back to work." Jackson disconnected the call. The phone rang almost immediately, but the teen ignored it when he saw Logan's name on caller ID.

Jackson spent the next hour perfecting the details for that night's presentation. Johanna would probably walk in, right in the middle of it. He froze. If the Terrorians were planning anything, all those poor little librarians would get caught in the crossfire. Talk about rotten timing. In his estimation, the library board had picked the worst possible night for a demonstration. *Maybe if I call the president of the board of directors, I can appeal to the man's better sense.* Jackson dialed the number and waited for the president's secretary to put him on the line.

"Is everything ready for tonight?"

No "Hello, Jackson, how are you?" No small talk of any kind—just a command disguised as a question.

"Sir, I'm thinking tonight is not the best night for

the presentation."

"Tonight is the perfect night for it. And it's the only night for it. Tell me, Jackson, do you *like* working at the library?" The teen shivered when he heard the thinly veiled threat with an icy-cold delivery.

"I only mentioned it because Johanna is returning tonight, and as curator, she'll be very disappointed she wasn't part of the event."

"That's what she gets for leaving town without notice." *Click.*

Jackson did not have time to react to the click, because someone started banging on the door. He checked the security camera and sighed. *Logan.* "Illumination." The door slid open.

"I had a devil of a time finding this place," Logan said. "I was sure I knew how to get here, but the streets all seemed to lead me in a different direction."

"Yeah, that happens," Jackson answered.

"So, why do you want a gun?"

"There may be some trouble here tonight. The library board wants me to give a demonstration, but some ... uh ... unsavory characters may show up."

"'Unsavory characters'? At this library? I think you're reading too many of these books and not spending enough time in the real world."

"You can't repeat that to anyone, you know. My job is on the line."

Logan knew how much Jackson's family depended on his paycheck—not that he made a lot of money, but every little bit helped. "Marcus Hurble."

"What about him?"

"I heard he has a couple of guns he wants to sell. That was last week. I didn't pay much attention, because I'm not interested in buying one. But he may still have one to sell. Do you want me to find out?"

"You can't tell anybody."

"Right. How much do you want to spend?"

Jackson counted the money in his wallet. It contained every cent he owned. He wanted to buy a car, and hoped by the time he turned eighteen he might be able to scrape together enough money to get a used one. He hated parting with his hard-earned cash, but if trouble broke out tonight and he wasn't prepared, he might not even be around for his eighteenth birthday. He counted out five hundred dollars. "Do you think this is enough?"

"How do I know?"

"Just make sure the gun works."

"I'm not shooting it."

"Well ... don't buy something you haven't heard of, you know?"

"So you want an UZI ..."

Jackson didn't answer.

"Fine. I'll be back as soon as I can."

"Ammo," the curator-in-training blurted out.

"You know if you load it, you can hurt someone."

"That's the idea."

JOHANNA HEARD NERO 51's footsteps fade as he headed toward the antechamber. She waited a few minutes, to allow him to become totally engrossed in whatever he was doing, before dashing up the spiral stairs and grabbing the cleaning supplies. She then scurried up the ladder to retrieve the protein bar she had hidden the day before.

"Looking for something?"

The sound of Nero 51's voice gave her chills. "Yes. I forgot my protein bar up here yesterday, and since you wouldn't let me to finish my lunch today, I need it to relieve my hunger."

He stared at her hands. "I don't see any such thing."

She reached behind the obelisks and pulled out the bar. "This."

"You are here to work, not to eat." He grabbed the protein bar and put it in his pocket. "I believe you were working downstairs."

"Yes."

"Take the ladder with you."

He obviously did not want her working on the second floor. *Maybe this is where he's hiding the fakes.*

JACKSON PACED IN wide circles around the circulation desk. It seemed like hours since Logan had left. The curator-in-training's stomach growled, but he didn't want to leave the library to get lunch, in case his friend returned while he was out. *Instead of a car, I should get a cell phone. Then I could text him.*

"Argh." He hit himself in the head for being so stupid. He picked up the phone on the circulation desk and dialed Logan's cell number. "Where are you?"

"Piccolo Italia. A guy's gotta have lunch."

"Good. Bring me a meatball hero. I'm starving. Did you have any luck with ... you know?"

"Yeah. I'll be there soon."

"Okay. Hurry."

The ticking of the grandfather clock drove Jackson crazy. It was still early, but he felt like every minute stretched into an hour. He had practically worn a groove in the floor by the time he heard Logan banging on the door. His friend carried two bags, a white one from the pizzeria and a brown one, which must have held the gun.

Logan handed him the white bag. "Eat while I tell you about my little jaunt into the world of handguns."

Jackson ripped the wrapper off his sandwich. "Spill."

"Marcus Hurble has been arrested."

"While you were there?"

"No. Last night. The cops say he robbed a church poor box. Mrs. Krebs, that little old lady who lives across the street from the rectory, told police she heard a gunshot and thought someone killed Reverend Blake. She claims she saw Hurble leaving the church. Reverend Blake is fine, but Hurble had a gun on him when the cops picked him up, so they charged him."

"I thought you said you got me a gun?"

"I did, but not from Hurble. I got it from Larry at Once A-Pawn A Time."

"That guy's a nut job. You didn't tell him it was for me, did you?"

"I told him it I needed it for target practice. He took down all my info ... or I guess I should say, my older brother's. If you ever shoot someone with this gun, he'll be the one they send up the river, and my life won't be worth a damn."

"So show me."

"Oh. And by the way, you owe me twenty bucks."

"It cost that much?"

"No," Logan answered, sliding a black case out of the bag and unlatching it. Inside, a 9mm Glock and an empty magazine sat embedded in the box's foam lining. "The gun was four hundred ninety-nine dollars. The ammo is what put you over the top."

Jackson inspected the Glock. "Did he show you how to use it?"

"It's a pawn shop, not a firing range. So no, he didn't show me how to use it."

"Did he at least show you how to load it?"

"No, because he didn't have any nine-millimeter rounds in stock. I had to go to Buy-Mart for that."

Jackson tensed. "Anybody could have seen you getting bullets at Buy-Mart. That's where my mother shops."

"It's Wednesday afternoon. Your mom is working. Everybody's mom is working. So you can stop working … up a sweat. Can I use the computer?"

"Why?"

"So we can find out how to load a gun you shouldn't own with bullets you shouldn't have."

"Go ahead."

Twenty minutes later, the gun was loaded and the safety was securely in place.

THE COLLEGE OF Overseers sat in an ancient chamber, considering their options.

⇌ *The girl has confirmed the existence of weapons.*

❖ *Yes.*

■ *Do we have evidence of the sale of antiquities?*

Ψ *No counterfeits have been reported.*

Σ *Our hands are tied.*

⚳ *The Terrorians will strike.*

π *We cannot prevent them from taking action.*

❋ *We do have options.*

§ *Yes.*

⇌ *We must turn on the resonator.*

★ *A visit to each of the realms is essential.*

⦿ *We will begin immediately, with the exception of Terroria. Plato Indelicat will travel there at the appointed time and escort the girl back to her own world.*

Ω *I do not see Pru Tellerence. Who will visit Dramatica?*

I will go to Dramatica. Stay illuminated, my

brethren.

It was time for Johanna's seven-hour rest period. Upon its completion, she would be escorted home. *Why can't they just let me go home now?* She thought it, but she didn't really mean it. She needed the time to look for counterfeits.

She listened carefully for the telltale signs of Nero 51's departure. She could barely hear the squeak of the front door from her room, but when the giant humidifier stopped churning, she knew for sure he had gone. She asked for sustenance, and quickly ate the potato-and-bean soup provided. The tankard contained lemon-flavored water, which she was glad of, because beer would have slowed her down. She noticed a light go on in the building across the courtyard. *That must be Building 7.* She would have to keep checking to make sure the light did not go out while she investigated the residence floor.

Two hours later, Johanna yawned. She had examined thousands of obelisks, and still hadn't found anything. Suddenly, she heard the humidifier fans sputter to life. She glanced across the vast opening in the center of the library and out the window. The light in Building 7 still burned. She dropped to the floor just as the front door opened, and dozens of Terrorians entered the library and headed toward her quarters.

Johanna did not hesitate. She stuffed the rag and paste in the back of the shelf and wriggled across the floor on her stomach. She heard feet slapping against steps as the Terrorians climbed the curator's staircase. Johanna rolled across the floor as fast as she could, straight into the old, stone stairwell adjacent to the front entrance.

She heard someone say, "Bli z' Bril." They were

apparently more interested in Nero 51's residence than her quarters.

She crept down the stairs, but remained hidden in the stairwell. If she crouched in the dimly lit corner, she could watch the main part of the library, unobserved. Before long, she saw a parade of Terrorians carry weapons out the main entrance. They walked in unified precision, as if one brain commanded everyone's movement. Only one Terrorian at the end of the line marched a hair out of step. *He won't last long,* she thought. *They'll probably execute him for missing a beat.* By the time the last of them exited, those who had been at the front of the procession returned to transport even more weapons. She knew the retrieval of arms had ended when the humidifier again went silent.

Johanna wanted to contact Mal, but first, she needed to clean up loose ends. She climbed the stairs, and tried to remember which shelf she had hidden the rag and paste on. She grabbed them in haste, clumsily knocking over an obelisk. If anyone had been in the library, they would have heard her gasp. She could not afford to break another crystal and incite the wrath of Nero 51. She looked at it lying on its side, unbroken. *Curious.*

She picked it up. It felt as heavy as the others, but not in the same way. She picked up a second obelisk and immediately knew it was real. The crystal was uniformly heavy. But all the weight of the unbroken figurine was in the base. *I'm such a fool.* She had probably picked up dozens of fakes, but disregarded them because they had felt as heavy as crystal. She took the counterfeit back to her room and got out Mal's diary.

"Mal, I found a fake obelisk. It looks like crystal, but I knocked it over by accident and it didn't break.

What should I do?"

His answer did not arrive for more than an hour.

Nothing. You are only there to serve your sentence.

Mal could be so exasperating. Surely she could do something. She grabbed her backpack and looked for her cell phone. Her battery had lost a lot of its juice, but she only needed enough power to take a few pictures. She photographed the obelisk from several different angles, so she could describe it in her diary, which she knew Mal read regularly. She also took several pictures of the weapon she had ... uh ... confiscated. *Stolen is such an ugly word.*

She didn't know what else she could do. She looked at her phone—6:00 a.m. In two more hours, it would be time to return home.

JACKSON SLIPPED THE loaded gun in his waistband, just like he had seen on TV. *I hope I don't shoot off any body parts. That would be embarrassing. And painful.* Everything was ready to go.

R-R-R-I-I-I-N-N-N-G-G-G! He answered the phone. "Library of Illumination."

"Yeah. I'm from Delectable Comestibles. You placed an order?"

"Yes."

"Could you open the front door? I've been standing here for fifteen minutes and still haven't figured out how to get in."

"Illumination." The wall slid open. "Right in here," Jackson said, leading the man to a table he had dragged up from the basement. He had considered using the circulation desk for serving coffee, but the television took up a lot of space.

While the man set out the refreshments, Jackson

switched on the TV to warm it up.

"That's it. Sign here." The caterer handed Jackson the invoice.

"Thanks." Jackson took a ten-dollar bill out of his pocket and tipped the guy. He was going broke as curator-in-training, and wished he had never pried open that stupid window.

THE SCREECHING SOUND of metal upon metal disrupted the silence in Libraries of Illumination on each of eleven worlds. Curators looked up to find their cupolas opening, and stared at the blinding light shooting up from their LOI medallions—straight through the sudden openings in their roofs. A moment later, the light went out as a member of the College of Overseers greeted each world's steward. Most of the curators expressed outrage when they learned Terrorians had stockpiled weapons and the threat of war was imminent.

HUNDREDS OF TERRORIAN soldiers amassed outside Building 7. They had been training all year for this moment, and were fired up. Nero 51 had promised them they would be handsomely rewarded for helping Terroria establish itself as the prime sovereign of the twelve literary worlds.

Inside Building 7, a quartermaster outfitted each Terrorian with a weapon and two crystals, one with their orders on it and another with a map of the library they were assigned to seize. The return of the Fantasian to her own world meant all the portals would be in a specific alignment, allowing the Terrorians to know which realm each portal would lead to.

In the courtyard, soldiers assembled into twelve flanks, with three leaders at the head of each. Nero 51 emerged from Building 7 and stood in the middle of a wide loggia facing them.

"Terrorians. For many millennia, our realm has waited patiently to reclaim its position as prime sovereign of the Libraries of Illumination. It is an honor we held for two millennia, only to have it snatched away by a united force of rabble-rousers who refused to recognize our indomitable spirit and natural ability to lead. Nine worlds against our one forced us to sacrifice our position of power, if not our dignity.

"It has long been my dream to restore our great world to its true destiny as leader of all Libraries of Illumination." Nero 51 smiled in the strangled way in which Terrorians contorted their faces to impart any semblance of benign cordiality. "To succeed in our endeavor, we must do something that at first may seem reprehensible, but is ultimately necessary. Your primary objective is the destruction of every piece of documented literature in each of the libraries, as soon as you have secured the site. Once the other library systems have been wiped clean of all knowledge, their outlying books and papers will cease to exist. Their records will be eradicated. They will be devoid of all facts, fiction, figures, histories, music, art, plans, manuals, maps—any and all information that has ever been recorded will cease to exist for them. The compendium of universal literature on Terroria will be the only surviving resource for all our worlds, and will provide us with the ultimate power to rule the others—consummate knowledge.

"Maul 232, take our 'fundraisers' to the cupola, immediately. May I remind you that this is supposed to be a social event, so mingle amiably. When the time comes, you will find weapons inside my residence.

"Advance teams, prepare to take your places. We

are moments away from glory. Use your weapons' force-field initiators to prevent our adversaries from detaining you. Humane conquest is the key to obtaining support. Those who yield to *our* ways will be *conditioned* to serve Terroria. However, there may be some who prefer to spill blood rather than accept the magnanimity of our governance.

"If you must, do not hesitate to use the Omicron Key." He turned a key on the side of his weapon and took aim at Heil 66. A black-and-white beam shot out of the armament, disintegrating the Terrorian. "Heil 66 claimed dedication to our cause, yet delayed giving me crucial information about a spy planted by the overseers in our library until just moments ago. He disregarded the prime directive, and has paid the ultimate price.

"If you must, eradicate all who resist."

—LOI—

LOI

CHAPTER NINE

OVERSEERS, EXCEPT PRU Tellerence and Plato Indelicat, arrived at their designated realms carrying large, flat boxes containing translucent screens. The overseers did their best to calm the librarians by discussing their precautions against the possibilities of what might occur, but without overwhelming success.

"How could you allow this to happen?" most curators asked.

𝔥 *We did not allow this to transpire. We simply did not prevent it.*

Their answer confused the curators. The overseers sought to distract them by asking their help to position the screens across from the portals. The shiny, paper-thin attachments easily adhered to the walls, and once in place, could not be detected.

"What will that do?" one curator asked.

𝔥 *It will make the Terrorians reflect on their*

actions.

"From what I've read about Terrorians, they're not a species that embraces reflection. They have more of a 'kill first, ask questions later' attitude."

🎵 *That, unfortunately, is accurate.*

JACKSON MOVED OUT of sight when he heard the cupola screech. Having witnessed it on Dramatica, he knew it meant the portals were opening. He should have been excited at the prospect of Johanna returning, but it was much too early. *If Terrorians are invading the library, I'm not going to be an easy target.* He slipped inside the coat closet and held his breath. Relief washed over him when he saw an overseer approach the circulation desk. Jackson walked out to greet him. "Where's Johanna?"

◍ *I am Selium Sorium. I'm here to assist in Johanna Charette's return.*

Someone pounding on the front door interrupted them. The overseer waved his hand, and the door slid open. The president of the library board of directors was on the other side, with his wife and a pair of librarians from a nearby village. The president stared at the overseer, then grabbed Jackson by the arm and pulled him out of earshot. "What the hell is this, a masquerade ball?"

Jackson pulled his arm away. "That man," he said, nodding at Selium Sorium, "is a very important member of this library's College of Overseers, and I suggest you don't insult him."

"If he's so important, why haven't *I* ever met him?"

Jackson felt momentarily bewildered until the answer formed in his consciousness. "You're in charge of development for the management and growth of the library. However, Mr. Sorium oversees its *literary* endowments. After all, there would be no library if there was no collection of literature."

As far as the board president was concerned, the word *endowment* was spelled M-O-N-E-Y. He glared at Jackson before he walked over to the elderly man in the odd costume and introduced himself.

Jackson smiled. *That should keep him out of my hair.* He turned to see a librarian lean over the top of the circulation desk and pick up a slender volume of *The Strange Case of Dr. Jekyll and Mr. Hyde.* It was a Level Two book that had just been returned that afternoon. "Excuse me," he said, as he rushed to her side and pulled the small book out of her hand before she could open it. "If you start reading that," he joked, "you'll never pay any attention to me. Why don't you find a seat up front? We'll be starting in just a minute."

"I was just looking for a little something to occupy my time."

Oh, it will keep you occupied, he thought. He stuffed the book in his jacket pocket and continued greeting guests, while keeping an eye on the crowd to make sure "curiosity did not kill the cat."

NERO 51 CHECKED his timepiece. It was time for Operation Final Darkness to commence. He raised his weapon into the air while pulling a sliding lever on its side, a feature not included on most of the other arms. Suddenly, everyone's weapon glowed with an eerie purple light.

"To the portals!" he cried.

THE LIBRARIANS IN the Fantasian reading room settled in for the presentation.

Selium Sorium nodded at Jackson.

The teen took his cue. "Good evening, everyone.

Are you ready to see how to convert your system into one that's designed for the twenty-first century?"

Some of the librarians applauded. One man shook his head and said out loud, "I hope this isn't a waste of time, because our system is already computerized." Other librarians whose organizations had also converted to computer nodded in agreement.

"I know most of you have already switched to online public-access catalogs. That's not what we're discussing. We're here to talk about wirelessly retrieving information from anywhere—a car, your back yard, or even a cruise ship at sea. Tonight, we're talking about serving our communities with cutting-edge technology. In today's society, the keyword is 'instant gratification.'"

Jackson used a remote control to bring the giant TV screen to life. It showed banks of library tables filled with sleek computers—with nary a book in sight. "These computers will access our library's full array of knowledge, as well as connect to online creative editing programs for video, photos, music, and text. We like to call it our 'digital hub.'" He took a deep breath. "And if we're very lucky, maybe we can talk the president of our board of directors into approving this." An image of a three-dimensional printer filled the screen.

Jackson saw the board president scowl, but forged ahead. "With our wireless and online capabilities *and* a 3-D printer, we can become *research central*—a think tank that fosters creativity, invention, and innovative solutions to take us into the future."

"What happens when your hard drive fails?" someone asked.

"Lock the doors," another person called out, inciting giggles and snickers.

"Here at the Library of Illumination, we save all

our information to multiple cloud servers, and retrieve it wirelessly using these." He waved an iPad in the air.

"Does that work when you've got no electricity or modem?" someone asked.

"It does if you have a mobile hot spot—which is easy enough to get."

The audience buzzed. Jackson grinned as he changed the slide and pointed to the screen. An image with a graphic about cloud computing appeared, and then pixilated before changing to video of a scary-looking alien with a huge weapon. Everyone laughed except Jackson and Selium Sorium, who immediately recognized a Terrorian soldier.

JOHANNA SAT ON the edge of her cot, wearing her backpack. Inside, she had packed the fake obelisk. She rebalanced the stolen Terrorian weapon, now braced against her shoulder. She almost abandoned her choice to use it when it started emitting a purple glow, but changed her mind when she heard the humidifiers roar to life.

The Terrorians embraced precision. Johanna had witnessed it when they marched in unison to recover the weapons stored in Nero 51's residence. It would not surprise her if the curator activated all the guns at the same time, resulting in the subtle purple light.

She took a deep breath. If anyone entered the room, other than an overseer, she planned to immobilize that person and everyone who followed. She didn't really know how the weapon worked, but it looked fairly straightforward; it had a wider end, a narrower end, and a double ring that reminded her of a partial eclipse, which she surmised was the trigger. She shivered not because she felt cold but because she was anxious. *What if this thing doesn't shoot? What if they execute me? Who will take care of the library? What about Jackson? Is that why they made him a curator-in-training, because they already knew I wouldn't be returning?*

Her door suddenly opened, and without thought she pulled the trigger, and the weapon fired.

ON EVERY REALM, Terrorian advance teams dove through the portals with their weapons at the ready. A scout on each team stepped forward to survey the open space that exposed each library's aboveground levels, looking for signs of resistance. A second member of the team covered the scout, while the third warrior stood guard over the portal. On the other side of the openings, troops began amassing, ready to launch into battle. They stood poised, awaiting the go-ahead from the advance teams.

In most cases, the libraries were quiet. However, some exceptions existed.

OPEL 29 WAS motivated by the possibility of confrontation. Like many members of his species, his eagerness manifested itself as secretions from overactive glands—much like sweat. He signaled his Terrorian partners that they should hold their positions until he got an idea of what they might be up against. He leaned over the cupola walkway and was instantly stunned by what he saw. *How can this be?* Below sat an army of Fantasians, waiting to take them on. He wiped excess secretions from his brow with a tentacle, which sent a hail of minuscule droplets onto the people below. One of them turned to look up, and Opel 29 immediately jerked back.

"Do YOU HAVE a sprinkler system in here? I think it's leaking," a librarian said.

Jackson took a deep breath. "I'll go see what it is."

"Wait," the overseer said in a normal voice, rather than transferring his thoughts inside everyone's head. "These people are interested in what you have to say. I will check on the upper level."

"No," the president of the board of directors declared. "If anyone's going to check on the condition of this library, I'll do it." He pushed past the overseer and headed toward the cupola stairs.

◍ *Oh, dear.*

Jackson could hear the overseer's thoughts in his head.

◍ *This has "catastrophe" written all over it.*

THE FORCE OF the blast from the Terrorian weapon threw Johanna forward. She collided with Plato Indelicat, who grabbed the young woman to steady her. The wall behind the cot glowed. The overseer moved to touch it.

Ω *You have enveloped the wall in a force field.*

"Delumination," Johanna stated. The force field continued to glow.

Ω *The Terrorians have obviously reconfigured the key to their force fields.*

"Bril," Johanna tried.

Ω *Bril means "illuminate," not "deluminate." Dril.*

The overseer's attempt failed.

Ω *As I have said, they have altered the code for deactivating the shield. Little matter. The Terrorians will deal with it when they come back. It is time to go to the portal.*

Johanna picked up the weapon and turned it around. "At least now I know which end to aim."

Plato Indelicat warily eyed the young woman.

Ω *Be illuminated, Johanna Charette. There will be Terrorians on your world.*

THE LEADER OF the Terrorian advance team assigned to Dramatica descended to the main floor of the library. He could hear Furst humming in the antechamber. He twirled a tentacle in an upward spiral, motioning the others to begin moving through the portals to the cupola. A dozen soldiers had crossed when the Terrorian scout heard Furst push back his chair. His tentacle suddenly dropped, and the troops stilled, awaiting further instruction.

The team leader stepped back behind a shelf.

Furst's humming got louder as he approached the main reading room, but then ended in a series of sniffs.

The team leader readied his weapon.

Furst rounded the corner, and then he spotted the Terrorian. His red, curly hair pulled into tight, wiry corkscrews, and he flexed his knees.

The Terrorian aimed his weapon.

That is ill-advised.

The words he heard did not deter the soldier from pulling the trigger.

ON EACH OF the worlds, curators experienced similar events. They had been instructed to go about their normal routines, while the overseers used an enchantment on themselves to shrink to the size of one of Johanna's protein bars. At that height, they looked more like figurines than people, and could often observe what was going on undisturbed. Even the curators disregarded the overseers' presence.

JACKSON FOUND IT difficult to concentrate as he continued his presentation to the librarians. He could hear the president stomping up the cupola staircase as it rose like a patinated metal helix through the five uppermost levels of the library. Every so often, the footsteps stopped as the president paused to catch his breath.

High above him, the Terrorians watched and waited, ready to suspend their first victim behind an impenetrable force field.

JOHANNA BEGAN TO exit her quarters but stopped when she heard countless troops of Terrorian soldiers stomping up the cupola stairs. She slammed the door to her chamber, with Plato Indelicat and herself still inside. "The Terrorians are all heading to the cupola. How will we get past them to the portals?"

Ω *We will wait. Terrorians are an impatient breed. They will waste no time traversing the portals to force their will on beings from other realms. Once they have done that, we will return to Fantasia.*

"But they'll already be there, doing lord knows what to my library."

Ω *I suggest you leave the weapon behind. There is the possibility that other Terrorians will follow. Being caught with one of their weapons could mean certain death. You would be perceived as a spy and never be allowed to leave this place. Without the weapon, you are merely a Fantasian who has served a sentence and is being escorted home. They will allow the charade to continue until you reach your home planet, just so they can relish your sudden realization of domination rather than escape.*

"How nice of them."

Ω *Come. The footsteps have ceased.*

They climbed to the cupola and made their way to the portal to Fantasia. They saw no sign of the Terrorians. The troops had all transported to the other libraries. Johanna took a deep breath and said, "Illuminate." When nothing happened, Plato Indelicat repeated the command, and the pair immediately transported to the other side.

ON TERRORIA, NERO 51 lifted a tankard of fermented merk. "T' cra!"

Members of his inner circle echoed his toast. "T' cra." *To victory.*

It would not be long before reports filtered in from the troops, declaring their positions and successes. Nero 51 used a tentacle to wipe the foamy head of the sudsy spirits from his mouth. His plan had been perfectly executed. Every man had been thoroughly trained and appropriately dispatched. One member of each advance team was fluent in the language of the realm being invaded. The timing had been perfect. The only imperfection scratching the smooth surface of his plan was Heil 66. He had been a member of the inner circle, and yet had withheld information about a spy. Nero 51 wanted to believe the shadow Heil 66 had seen belonged to Johanna Charette, but the information had come too late to interrogate the girl. *What if someone else spied on me?* It made Nero 51 uneasy.

"I am going to withdraw in preparation for victory," he told the others. He handed them a small black box with three buttons. "Please buzz me when you have heard from our soldiers on every world. Press the white button for total victory, the purple button for partial victory, and the red button for retreat."

"So fancy, Nero 51. Why not just have us meet you at the library when we hear from the troops?"

"I will be contemplating victory and fine-tuning our plans for the future—in a place of meditation. It will be easier to contact me in this manner." He raised one of his right tentacles. "T' cra!" He worked his way toward the exit, entwining tentacles with each member of his inner circle in a show of solidarity.

Back inside his library, Nero 51 descended to the basement and moved the bookcase leading to the sub-levels. Like all the Libraries of Illumination, his had been designed with 1,311 floors, most of them underground. However, he had taken the initiative to create a secret passage on level 333 that led to a living compartment only he knew about. He had used it as his personal residence for years, and had stocked it well, with everything he could possibly need. He preferred to use his official quarters on the residence level as a command post. It was the perfect place to store munitions and pertinent information about the invasion, to keep them close at hand.

He settled into a comfortable position and looked at the bank of lights near the ceiling, white, purple, and red. He could relax here, undisturbed, while remaining informed about Terrorian exploits on distant realms. He closed his eyes and sank into deep meditation.

—LOI—

LOI

CHAPTER TEN

"What the ...?"

Even before the president of the board of directors had finished his sentence, a Terrorian trooper took aim and fired his weapon. The blast caused a high-pitched squeal that reverberated throughout the library and caused the president, as well as Jackson and their guests on the main floor, to slump over or drop to the ground, cover their ears, and suffer the pain. The pitch of the audio signal had a much different effect on the Terrorian who fired his weapon. It caused the weapon to reverse action, locking the shooter in a force field.

The other soldiers did not immediately comprehend what had happened to their team leader. Instead, they saw the president of the library board still moving, so several of them took aim and fired.

Terrorians began freezing in place, unable to move after firing their weapons. One of the remaining soldiers threw his weapon down and raced down the stairs, intent on strangling any Fantasians he met with his bare tentacles.

JACKSON STRUGGLED UP from the floor, even though his ears continued to ring. If Johanna returned now, he feared she would get caught in the crossfire. He raced up the stairs to the cupola, only to find his way blocked by a Terrorian. The soldier extended his tentacles, as Jackson stepped back and reached into his waistband. The teen removed the gun and fired a shot before the Terrorian knocked the Glock out of his hand and it clattered down the long staircase. The bullet hit the Terrorian, and a spray of blood covered Jackson in a purple haze. The soldier squealed in pain, but did not give up.

Another tentacle snaked toward Jackson. He stuffed his hand in his jacket pocket, looking for a screwdriver or pen—anything he could use as a weapon. His fingers closed over the slender volume of *The Strange Case of Dr. Jekyll and Mr. Hyde*, and he pulled out the book.

The Terrorian knocked it out of his hand, but Mr. Hyde suddenly sprang from the pages of the open book, carrying a heavy cane with a blood-covered handle. He used it to beat the startled Terrorian until the soldier went limp. Jackson ducked, grabbed the book, and quickly closed it. He slipped it back in his pocket before he climbed over the inert soldier and continued up the stairs.

THE LAST FEW troopers on Fantasia realized their weapons had been turned against them and tried to retreat, but the portal suddenly flashed, and Plato Indelicat and Johanna appeared.

Without thinking, one of the soldiers fired his weapon, causing Johanna to drop to the ground, writhing from the pitch of audio feedback. The warrior immediately found himself locked behind a force field. His fellow soldiers dropped their weapons, grabbed the overseer, and jumped back through the portal to Terroria. They dragged Plato Indelicat through their library, out onto the toxic streets of the Twelfth Realm, and into Building 7—a location that they felt would give them greater control over their hostage.

Members of the Inner Circle grew disturbed when they heard about the defeat of their plan, but remained hopeful that a hostage would aid their negotiations with the College of Overseers.

TROOPS ON OTHER realms reported similar outcomes. Soldiers found themselves suddenly immobilized by force fields. A warrior in the Numericon library switched on his weapon's Omicron Key and was vaporized when he fired at Pi, curator of the Tenth Realm. The few Terrorian troopers who managed to retreat all had similar tales to tell.

JACKSON QUICKLY RECUPERATED from the second earsplitting blast, and reached the cupola in time to see Johanna recover from the effects of the Terrorian weapons. He helped her off the ground and slipped his arms around her, glad to see she was okay.

She pushed him away. "I've got to save Plato Indelicat," she screamed, and disappeared back through the portal.

His mouth hung open—just for a moment. He leaned over the cupola railing and yelled to the crowd below: "Tonight's demonstration has been canceled due to unforeseen technical difficulties. Please exit in an orderly fashion." Then he jumped through the portal.

ON TERRORIA, JOHANNA's footsteps pounded down the cupola stairs. Jackson followed as fast as he could, often taking two steps at a time to catch up to her. He saw her run into a utility closet and reemerge with a weapon.

"You can't shoot that," he said. "You'll end up caught in a force field."

Johanna studied the gun. "Did the overseers do anything strange before the Terrorians arrived?"

"Yeah. They stuck a bunch of shiny white papers on the walls by the portals, but they had nothing on them. You couldn't even see them."

"That high-pitched tone ... did you hear that when Nero 51 grabbed you outside his residence and put you in a force field?"

Jackson shook his head. "No."

"Okay. I'm thinking those shiny white papers had something to do with the way the guns backfired. But I'm also thinking the overseers wouldn't have bothered sticking them here on Terroria, where they might have been discovered. So this weapon is probably going to work just the way we expect it to."

"If you say so. Do you think the overseer is here? I don't hear anyone."

Johanna ran to a window and looked over at Building 7. "No, but I bet I know where they took him. Follow me."

The two of them ran into the street, but immediately retreated, coughing and gagging. "What is that smell?" Jackson moaned.

"I don't know. I never strayed outside of the library. I only know that every time the Terrorians entered, they'd turn on a blower that makes a real racket. That's how I knew when Nero 51 was in residence."

"Is there some kind of secret passageway to the building you want to go to?"

"Nope. We've got to go out there, but it's just across the courtyard. We can hold our breath that long."

"Right. We deplete our oxygen supply while we run into a building that's full of armed Terrorians, with a weapon that may backfire."

She nodded. "Pretty much."

"Okay. Let's do it."

They both took a deep breath and headed out.

SELIUM SORIUM MADE sure everyone who had attended Jackson's presentation left the building safely. The president of the board of directors babbled about being attacked by some "armed monstrosity," but the overseer convinced everyone that the man had hit his head when he fell. He encouraged the president's wife to have her husband checked for a concussion.

Finally alone, the overseer closed his eyes to commune with his brethren. Ten of his colleagues gave positive reports on the worlds they observed; however, they now knew Plato Indelicat had been taken hostage.

That is a setback.

The overseers possessed supernatural powers that enabled them to communicate, transport themselves, and alter the perception of their appearance. They had also undergone a special longevicus ritual to extend their lives tenfold. As the guardians of all knowledge, they relied on those gifts to maintain their existence. However, the overseers were not immortal. The Original Thirteen, save one, had passed on. Overseers could be fatally injured, and Plato Indelicat would have to use his wits wisely to continue his state of being.

JOHANNA AND JACKSON heard the pandemonium erupting inside Building 7 before they even reached the door. They hid in the shadows as someone exited, and saw a cloakroom just inside the vestibule. A diminutive Terrorian, possibly a woman or a child, appeared to be in charge of it. The discussion in the main hall became more and more heated, and the tiny Terrorian got up and joined the crowd to get a better look.

"Come on." Johanna pulled Jackson inside the grimy cloakroom.

"It smells almost as bad in here as it does outside," he whispered.

"Yeah. This is what Terrorians smell like. And if we smell like them, they may not notice us." She grabbed a cloak from the corner and threw it over her shoulders, covering the weapon. She pulled the hood over her hair and tugged it down to conceal her face.

Jackson did the same. "There are no arm holes."

"Look again. There are four on each side—they're just smaller—for tentacles."

The teens moved out of the coatroom but stayed in the shadows near the door. Most of the Terrorians, by contrast, pushed forward to get right into the middle of the discussion.

"Did you learn any more Terrorian here?" Jackson whispered.

"No. Plato Indelicat performed a translation enchantment so I would be able to understand the Terrorians when they ordered me around."

"So everything was in English?"

"Everything except the passphrase to get into the residence."

"Did you figure it out?"

"Lucky for me, someone taught it to me before I started my sentence."

"Who did that?" he asked, amazed.

"You."

The roar of the crowd increased, and a pair of Terrorian soldiers marched Plato Indelicat to the front of the room.

Jackson leaned toward Johanna. "It sounds like a freakin' cricket convention."

"I wish we knew what they were saying." She stared at Plato Indelicat, trying to read his face. A moment later, an English translation enchantment took effect.

"What did you do?" Jackson whispered.

"He knows we're here. He must have read our thoughts."

MANY OF THE younger Terrorians called for Plato Indelicat's execution. Older residents claimed they needed him as a hostage to use as a bargaining chip. With Plato Indelicat incarcerated on Terroria, the possibility that they could exchange the overseer for the troops who remained immobilized in force fields on distant worlds still existed. But more importantly, the portals might remain open, keeping the hope of a future victory alive.

A Terrorian soldier interrogated the overseer about why their weapons had backfired. Plato Indelicat did not answer his questions. A nearby soldier picked up a weapon and swung it at the overseer. He swung high, and the weapon knocked Plato Indelicat's hat off his head.

The overseer suddenly grew agitated, and struggled to pull away from the soldiers who held him in place, but they kept a firm grip on him. Another soldier stuck his weapon inside the hat and raised it above his head—a symbol of their small victory in capturing the overseer. The crowd cheered, barely noticing that Plato Indelicat had started to wither.

Johanna turned to Jackson. "We've got to do something before the Terrorians tear him to pieces."

"What do you suggest?"

"I don't know, but we'd better act soon."

Someone shouted a command from the center of the crowd. "We must take him to Nero 51. He'll know what do."

"Where is Nero 51?" a soldier asked.

"Planning our future path to victory in the Library of Illumination. We must take the prisoner to the library."

"Let's get out of here," Johanna said. "We've got a better chance of saving Plato Indelicat in the library than we do here."

"How do you figure that?"

"We know the lay of the land. They'll be afraid to shoot their guns in there. And the portals are nearby."

"So all we've got to do is run up five noisy flights of ancient stairs with an old man in tow? Piece of cake."

They slipped out of Building 7 with the crowd and made their way to the library. Inside, Johanna grabbed Jackson and dragged him into the corner of the stone stairwell.

"We'll be safer in here," she whispered.

On the other side of the wall, the mob got restless when Nero 51 did not answer the bell they used to summon him.

"The box," a member of the Inner Circle said. "Where is the box he gave us?"

Another member held it up. "I have it right here."

"Good. Press the button."

"Which one?"

"Well, we weren't completely victorious, so don't press the white one."

"Do you think I should press the purple one for partial victory?"

"Uhhh ... We haven't really taken control of any of the libraries. The few troops who have returned—retreated."

"So you think I should press the red button?"

"That would be the most accurate assessment of what has happened. He deserves to know that."

The Inner Circle member pressed the red button, and almost immediately Building 7 exploded, blowing out the windows on one side of the library and shaking the structure to its core. Stunned Terrorians squealed as they dove for cover.

"Now!" Johanna said, and ran into the fray, grabbing Plato Indelicat and dragging him to the cupola steps.

Jackson followed close behind her. They began running up the stairs, but the overseer's robe, his advanced years, and his delicate condition slowed them down.

"Can you carry him?" she asked. Jackson threw the overseer over his shoulder like a bag of laundry, and Johanna pushed him ahead of her. "Run," she cried.

A RED LIGHT blinked on sub-level 333. Nero 51 rose in a rage. What could his troops have done to lead to total defeat? He felt the subterranean cavity he had built shudder. *Building 7 has been destroyed. It serves them right for ruining my plan.*

THE EXPLOSION STUNNED the Terrorians. Some were knocked unconscious by the percussion, but a few raised their heads in time to see *aliens* grab the overseer and drag him away. Many Terrorians felt defeated and did not rush to pursue the interlopers, but a few seized the moment, believing the aliens had bombed Building 7 and were now escaping with Terroria's hostage. They clambered up the stairs, their fat, flat feet slapping the metal treads.

JACKSON WAS STRONG, but rushing up five flights of narrow, spiral stairs carrying a man over his shoulder took its toll. He could feel the Terrorian pursuers. Their added weight on the staircase made it shudder. He hoped that whatever held the stairway in place had been designed to withstand the weight load.

"They're gaining on us," Johanna shouted. "Can you go any faster?"

"No." He knew it wasn't the answer she wanted to hear, but he had to tell her the truth.

"Here goes nothing," she said, as she turned and raised the Terrorian weapon to her shoulder. She barely had time to aim before she pulled the trigger. A force field encased the closest Terrorian, blocking the ones who followed. She turned and ran, catching up to Jackson and Plato Indelicat at the portals.

"Illuminate," Jackson yelled.

Nothing happened.

Johanna echoed his command. "Illuminate!"

The portals remained closed.

"Plato," she cried. The overseer was unconscious. She gently tapped his cheek. "Please, Plato, you've got to help us. How do we open the portals?"

The overseer's eyes fluttered. He mumbled something difficult to understand.

"What is he saying?"

Johanna looked confused. "I think he said, 'The

key is in the might.'"

"What does that mean?" Jackson asked.

"I don't know, but I hear them coming up the stairs, so they must have gotten around the soldier I shot.

"Please, Plato," she begged. "There must be a word that will open the portals."

He looked at her through clouded, gray eyes.

Ω *Totalis illuminatio.*

Instantly, they transported to their own world, where Selium Sorium met them.

◍ *Totalis tenebris.*

The portals slammed shut.

"We saved him," she cried triumphantly.

◍ *He will be laid to rest with those who have come before.*

"What are you talking about?" Jackson gently placed Plato Indelicat on the floor.

◍ *He is no more.*

"You mean, he's dead? He can't be dead. We saved him," Jackson stated.

Johanna's face clouded over. "How could he die?"

◍ *We are grateful that his body has been returned to us. You have provided a great service, Johanna Charette. And you, Jackson Roth.*

"How can you say that? Why don't you help him?" She suddenly felt empty inside.

◍ *You have provided us with information about Terrorian arms and confirmed violations against the Library of Illumination through the illegal trade of precious artifacts.*

Jackson looked around at the Terrorians still suspended behind force fields. "What about them?"

◍ *They will be taken to Lumina for trial.*

"So the portals are still open?"

◍ *We have effectively sealed them for now.*

Johanna's brow furrowed. "How will you get to Lumina?"

◍ *Like this.*

Selium Sorium, the body of Plato Indelicat, and more than a half dozen Terrorian soldiers disappeared.

Johanna and Jackson looked around in astonishment, and then at each other.

"It's over," Jackson said, as he wrapped her in his arms and gave her a bear hug. "It's over," he repeated, "and you're home."

Tears streamed from her eyes, and she began to sob.

"Don't cry." Jackson rubbed her back. "You helped avert a war. You did everything in your power to rescue an overseer. You survived! You should be overjoyed by your accomplishments. And then there's your crowning achievement."

"What's that?" She looked up at him.

"I will never, ever again say, 'I bet there's something hidden behind this wall.'"

She smiled, but she could not shake the sensation of doom she felt. The Terrorians had been planning an all-out war, and she didn't think they would easily abandon their plan.

To the contrary, whatever Johanna and Jackson had unwittingly become embroiled in had just begun.

—THE END, IT IS NOT—

Turn the page for a preview of the next
Library of Illumination adventure ...

THE OVERSEERS

Coming soon from Artiqua Press

LOI

THE OVERSEER

"THAT'S THE LAST of them," Jackson said with finality, as he pushed a stack of books toward Johanna. "Once you've read these, you'll know everything there is to know about the realm of Terroria. Although why you want to become an expert on *planet evil* is beyond me."

Johanna shook her head. "That's why I'm the curator and you're just my assistant."

"Hey, hey, hey, didn't you hear what they said when we stood trial for breaching the portals? I'm a *curator-in-training*. I'm the one waiting in the wings to pick up the pieces."

"Well then, you'd better read some of these, too," she said as she pushed the pile of Terrorian history books she'd already read, towards him. "Then we'll both be prepared."

"Prepared for what?"

"I'm not sure." She felt her nerve endings jitter. "But it never hurts to be prepared. You never know what can happen."

As if on cue, the middle of the venerable library began to wobble and shimmer, like the air that hovers above a hot roadway on a steamy summer day. Suddenly, a 22nd century time machine appeared. It was the same one that Johanna's predecessor Mal had used to transport Casanova back to 18th century Venice, after the legendary lover suddenly popped out of a book in the library, and stayed. Mal smiled as he stepped out. His appearance had changed in the short weeks since Johanna and Jackson had last seen him.

"Are you growing a beard?" Johanna walked over to her mentor and gave him a hug. Mal had been in charge of the library for nearly four hundred years, and had only relinquished his stewardship after he had personally trained Johanna to deal with the intrusions, oddities and aftermath of *living* literature.

Mal stroked his face and smiled. "It was a little itchy at first, but I'm getting used to it now."

"It makes you look older," she observed.

"Yeah," Jackson said. "You used to look four-hundred and thirty years old and now you look four-hundred and thirty-one."

"Don't listen to him." Johanna placed her arm protectively around Mal's shoulder. "You don't look a day over eighty."

Mal smiled. "I come with sad news, and with happy news."

"I think the actual saying is, 'I have some good news and some bad news,'" Jackson quipped.

Mal slowly inhaled. "Sadly, we will say our final goodbyes to Plato Indelicat tomorrow, when he will be enshrined following a celebration of his life and a memorial to his death. On a more positive note, his replacement will be inducted into the College of Overseers on the following afternoon."

"Will anyone ever be able to take his place?" Johanna wondered out loud.

"Where do overseers come from anyway?" Jackson asked. "Is there a special place filled with them, like *Overseers-R-Us*? Do they have to supply their own hats? I know Plato Indelicat was pretty sad after the Terrorians knocked his pope hat off his head."

Mal's eyes grew more focused. "Can you tell me what became of Plato Indelicat's headpiece?"

Jackson shook his head. "Not really."

"We were too busy trying to stay ahead of the crowd," Johanna added. "They had turned into a lynch mob and we didn't want to become hostages, too."

"So it remains on Terroria."

"Unless it was destroyed in the explosion."

"Yeah," Jackson agreed. "The last place we saw it was in the building around the corner from the library, and that place was blown to smithereens, which was really good for us, because that's how we escaped."

Johanna took Mal's hand. "So, what's the happy news, Mal?"

"I've been selected as one of the candidates for the vacant overseer position."

"*One* of the candidates," Johanna noted. "Who are the others?"

"Well, of course, you wouldn't know them

because they're from other worlds, but there's Prophet IAN c. from Adventura, who is the current library curator, there. You may have met Torran, the head of the Library Council on Dramatica, who has declared himself a contender although I don't know how good *his* chances are. And then there's Dame Erato, the former curator of Romantica, who relocated to Lumina and has reinvented herself as something of an inspirational insider. She and Prophet IAN c. are both strong competitors."

"Do you think you have a chance?" Jackson asked.

"I have my strengths. But ultimately, it will be whomever the overseers believe brings the most needed assets to the college at this point in time. Whether that resource is political, administrative, militaristic or inspirational remains to be seen.

"There will be a challenge among the four of us, and any others who choose to declare themselves by noon tomorrow. I was hoping the two of you would remain after the memorial service to cheer me on."

"We're invited to Plato Indelicat's memorial service?" Johanna's eyes widened.

"Of course," Mal answered. "That's why I'm here."

Jackson nodded solemnly. "Cool."

"I've got to stay behind and take care of the library, Mal," Johanna sighed. "We can't both be gone at the same time."

"The library will be closed. All the Libraries of Illumination will cease operations for two days as a sign of respect for Plato Indelicat, and will not reopen until a new overseer has been sworn in."

"That seals the deal for me," Jackson said with a smile.

"Where is this all happening?" Johanna asked.

"Everything takes place on Lumina."

Of course it would; where else could it be held? Still, she was surprised that she and Jackson were invited. "The overseers sealed the portals after the Terrorians tried to take over the libraries. How will we get there if the portals are sealed?"

"I will escort you both."

"In that?" Jackson asked, not trying to hide his excitement.

"Absolutely. There's nothing like traveling in a time machine." Mal wiggled his eyebrows and grinned.

Jackson entered the time machine and looked around. "It's like standing inside a bubble." There was no floor, no doors and no visible controls. He touched the surface. It was firm, and warm, and as smooth as glass.

Johanna idly began straightening out the circulation desk. "Why would we need a time machine at all, if we're traveling in the present?"

"Because, it will take us back to a time when the portals were *open* so we can travel to Lumina, and then zigzag us back to the present." He tapped on the outside of the bubble twice, and exchanged places with Jackson. "I'll be back tomorrow morning at ten sharp." He pointed a finger at the *curator-in-training*, then laughed and shook his head, lowering his finger. "You won't be late."

"You've got that right," Jackson answered. "I'll get here by nine, so I don't miss anything."

Mal waved. The air around the time machine seemed to melt for a second before it disappeared.

"Lumina," Jackson said in awe. We've been to three realms, including our own, and now we're going to

Lumina. I'd never even been out of the country before we discovered the portals, but now I'll be traveling off world for the third time. How cool is that?"

"We're going to a funeral, and then Mal's challenge. It's not like we're attending a big rock concert on New Year's Eve."

"I know, but it's still the most amazing thing that has ever happened to me." He shrugged one shoulder and leaned over to kiss her. "Actually, you're the 'most amazing' thing that ever happened to me. If you had never come to the school and asked me if I wanted to work in the library, I'd probably be tossing pizzas at Piccolo Italia. Free pizza is nice, but not as nice as traveling to other realms with you.

He pushed the books on Terroria aside. "Do you think we have any books downstairs on Lumina? I think I'd like to study up on that world, before we leave tomorrow."

"Sometimes, you surprise me," Johanna laughed.

He winked at her. "Refreshing, isn't it?"

THERE WERE PLENTY of books about Lumina, as well as pictures, and Jackson was enthralled by everything he read. "I can't believe most of their world is covered in water."

"I don't know if it's most of the world. The cities are built on numerous outcroppings that jut way above the surface."

"Yeah, but look at this picture of the capital. The bottom of that giant *outcropping* looks like it rests on legs. The middle is open and I bet you can sail a tanker right through it."

"Kind of like a subway traveling under a city."

"No, this is way cooler than a subway. Besides, anyone riding in a subway would drown unless by subway you mean submarine."

"The golden city on top of the rocks makes it look so ethereal." Johanna ran her finger across a picture in *Lumina: Past and Present*. Instantly, a miniature three-dimensional version of the capitol city of Lumi appeared, complete with clouds above and water below.

Jackson moved closer and stared at a rock leg supporting the city. "Look. This one has a door."

Johanna walked over to see what he was talking about. "I would have loved this as a kid. What a perfect dollhouse. I never owned one, but I saw one once in a museum and I thought it was the most wonderful thing in the world."

As they watched, a round wooden tub with a dozen oarsmen sitting around its radius rowed up to the tiny entrance. One of the oarsmen unlocked the door and a group of tiny Luminans climbed out of the tub and disappeared inside, allowing the door to slam shut with a resounding thud.

"Can you believe this?" Jackson laughed.

Johanna started to laugh but instead, gasped. As they watched, a group of men appeared from under the surface of the water, swam up to the tub, and began pulling at the oars and tossing them away, so the oarsmen wouldn't be able to row. The tiny sailors grappled with their attackers, but one by one, many of them were pulled under the water. A few managed to hang onto their oars and moved into the middle of the tub where they used them to fight off their assailants. One attacker hoisted himself onto the vessel and soon learned he had made a big mistake.

"Holy... frit. Look at him," Jackson cried. "He's a fish!"

Johanna squinted. "I think the correct term is a *merman.*"

"Like Ethel Merman, the singer those guys at *The Comedy Club* are always impersonating?"

"No. Like the male equivalent to a mermaid."

"I knew that."

"Um hmm."

While they were talking, the oarsmen beat the brazen merman to a pulp, and pushed his body overboard—a sign of what other underwater creatures could expect, if they were thinking of hijacking a boat. The attack was over and in a single blink, the bodies of the fallen oarsmen and the beaten merman all disappeared under the surface of the murky water.

Johanna slammed the book shut. "I could have done without that."

"Yeah. But this isn't a storybook. It's a textbook that describes how things are on Lumina. And apparently, everything isn't fun and games in the golden city."

"Let's just hope we don't have to travel anywhere on the water while we're there."

B-R-R-R-I-I-I-N-N-N-G-G-G!

A phone call from *Book Services* informed them they had just received a scholarly request for research information and ancient texts. The order kept Johanna and Jackson busy for the rest of the afternoon. When they were done, Johanna sent Jackson home. She needed a little time to pack. Besides, she didn't want to start talking about Lumina again. She was still feeling uneasy about the attack they had witnessed when the book came to life, and it reminded her about the potential for an attack by Terrorians, if any of them were actually invited to the memorial service. She hoped not, but that wasn't her decision to make. The thought of running into Nero 51 again turned a trip that should be meaningful and interesting into a duty that filled her with dread.

THAT NIGHT, AS Johanna snuggled under the duvet in her bedroom, she opened Mal's diary and asked him if Nero 51 would also be on Lumina. Except for the time when she was serving her sentence on Terroria, Mal's answers to her requests had always been immediate, but tonight she dozed off waiting for his reply. When she awakened in the middle of the night, he still had not answered her. She glanced over at her clock. It was two in the morning. She had asked Mal her question more than three hours ago. He had never taken so long to respond. Johanna dozed off again, but continued to wake up every hour or so to check for Mal's answer. At 7:00 a.m. she threw off the covers and arose for the day. A quick check told her that Mal still hadn't answered her question.

She selected a long tan and black chevron print sweater and paired it with a short black skirt and black boots. She studied herself in the mirror. *Funeral attire.* She added a belt and a scarf. *Stylish funeral attire.* She packed something more lighthearted for the induction ceremony for the new overseer, as well as extra clothing to relax in. And then she waited. It was still too early for Mal to show up, although Jackson was probably on his way.

She grabbed Mal's diary to see if he had finally answered her question, but the last page of the diary remained blank. She threw the book in her bag and sighed. The library was closed and she was all packed and ready to go, and now she was forced to wait. She did the only thing left that felt natural. She paced.

A HALF-HOUR LATER, the back door flew open and Jackson breezed in. "I know I'm late, but I really needed to eat something, so I stopped to pick up some coffee and donuts. Unfortunately, everyone in town had the same idea. I thought of saying 'screw it,' but who knows when we'll get to eat again?"

Johanna was staring at him. "Is that a tie?"

"Yeah. You like it?" He stroked the narrow strip of black leather with pride. Jackson wore it over a light blue shirt and khakis. Everything else he needed was in the backpack slung over his shoulder.

"I don't think I've ever seen you wear a tie before."

"I don't think I've ever owned a tie before. I bought this one on my way home last night. It's *real* leather."

She gently touched the black leather and then straightened out the knot. "You look very nice. I like it."

He grinned. "Now all I have to do is make sure I don't spill any coffee on myself. Just to be safe, I didn't buy any jelly or cream-filled donuts. Why take chances?"

"Why, indeed?" She removed a plain cruller from the bag of treats. They chatted amiably until the grandfather clock struck ten. Johanna gulped down her coffee and used her hand to sweep the donut crumbs into the paper bag. "Mal will be here any second."

Jackson wasn't eager to rush through his morning

meal and took his time as Johanna fussed. The minutes ticked by. When he was done, he threw his coffee cup and crumbs in the trash bag, and then brought it out back to the dumpster. The clock was chiming the quarter hour when he returned.

Johanna frowned. "He's late."

"So the guy got hung up. Maybe he's making an 'under the counter' deal for the transport of human cargo.'"

Johanna didn't answer.

"That's what Mal said when he picked up Casanova. Don't you remember? He said he had to bargain with the people at Lloyds of London?"

"Don't you understand? Mal is always punctual. He's very dependable. His schedule runs like clockwork. But then, last night, he didn't answer a question I asked his diary. And now he's late. Something's wrong."

Jackson studied her face. She looked like she was on the verge of tears. He pulled her into a hug. "Don't worry. It won't matter if he's late. It's a *time machine,* and no matter what time he gets here, we can travel back to the perfect moment in time to go through the portals."

He rubbed her back to calm her and slowly felt her start to relax, but she grew tense again, when the clock chimed the half-hour.

—LOI—

THE REALMS OF THE
LIBRARIES OF ILLUMINATION

❖ Lumina   The Primary Realm   OO
       Master: Ryden Mmyrdis

⚕ Romantica   Realm O1
       Dean: Horatio Blastoe
       Curator: Natalia Dalura

Σ Adventura   Realm O2
       Dean: Artemus Rexana
       Curator: Prophet IAN c.

⇌ Educon   Realm O3
       Dean: Grappho Pluck
       Curator: Dr. Infinitis

❋ Scientico   Realm O4
       Dean: Galio Abbingdon
       Curator: Galon Senter

§ Juvenia   Realm O5
       Dean: Zenith Fullova
       Curator: Peer Meap

★ Dramatica   Realm O6
       Dean: Pru Tellerance
       Curator: Furst

☋ Comedia   Realm O7
       Dean: Reichel Bean
       Curator: Abbello Abbato

■ Inspiracon   Realm O8
       Dean: Marsh Kierand
       Curator: Issiopia

Ψ Mysteriose   Realm O9
       Dean: Proteus Bligh
       Curator: Hu, the Elder

π Numericon   Realm 1O
       Dean: Rubicon Zenicon
       Curator: Pi

◍ Fantasia   Realm 11
       Dean: Selium Sorium
       Curator: Johanna Charette

Ω Terroria   Realm 12
       Dean: Plato Indelicat
       Curator: Nero 51

℥ Consensus of All

ABOUT THE AUTHOR

C. A. Pack is the author of *Code Name: Evangeline* and the *Evangeline's Ghost* series, as well as the series of novelettes that make up *The Library of Illumination*. She is currently working on *The Second Chronicles of Illumination,* recounting the War of the Realms.

The author is an award-winning journalist, and former assignment manager/anchor at *LI News Tonight* in New York, and has worked as a news writer at WNBC-TV, and Cablevision's News 12 Long Island.

A member of International ThrillerWriters, and Sisters in Crime, she is also a former president of the Press Club of Long Island. She lives in Westbury, NY, with her husband, a couple of picky parrots, and dozens of imaginary characters who are constantly demanding page space.